A BIRD ON WATER STREET

WRITTEN AND ILLUSTRATED BY

ELIZABETH O. DULEMBA

Little
Pickle
Press

Published by Little Pickle Press, an imprint of Sourcebooks Jabberwocky
P.O. Box 4410, Naperville, Illinois 60567–4410
(630) 961-3900
sourcebookskids.com

Originally published in 2014 by Little Pickle Press.

Library of Congress Cataloging-in-Publication Data is on file with the publisher.

Source of Production: Versa Press, East Peoria, Illinois, USA
Date of Production: August 2019
Run Number: 5016175

Printed and bound in the United States of America.
VP 10 9 8 7 6 5 4 3 2 1

Praise for *A Bird on Water Street*

Parents' Picks Award, 2018 Winner

Volunteer State Book Awards, 2016-2017 Nominee

Georgia Children's Book Award, 2015-2016 Finalist

Georgia Author of the Year, 2015 Winner

Southern Independent Booksellers Association
(SIBA), 2014 Spring Okra Pick

The SIBA Book Award, 2015 Long List

Georgia Center for the Book, 2015 Books
All Young Georgians Should Read

Mom's Choice Awards, 2014 Gold Award Winner

Moonbeam Children's Book Awards, 2014 Gold Award Winner

eLit Awards, 2014 Gold Medal Winner

The Green Earth Book Award, 2014 Honor Book

Academics' Choice Award, 2014 Smart Book Award

Foreword Reviews INDIES Book of the Year,
2014 Finalist for Juvenile Fiction

The 2014 National Book Festival Featured Title for Georgia

"A little-known but important chapter in United States history springs to life. As big-hearted and joyful as it is sobering, this book should be required reading for students studying the impact of man upon the environment. I will never take a sparrow—or bug—for granted again."

—Lynn Cullen, bestselling author of *Mrs. Poe*

"Elizabeth Dulemba seamlessly melds a coming-of-age story to the reality of life in a single-industry town. This is a book that sings."

—Betsy Bird, author of *Giant Dance Party* and the *School Library Journal* children's literary blog, *A Fuse #8 Production*

"A riveting look at life in a copper-mining Tennessee town where nature has been savaged into a moonscape and the air burns holes through laundry left on the line. Jack leaps off the page as a boy determined to keep his father safe from the mines and bring living things back to his home."

—Vicky Alvear Shecter, author of *Cleopatra's Moon* and *Anubis Speaks!*

To
Grace Postelle (June 25, 1926–October 29, 2010),
Doris Abernathy (November 27, 1927–),
the citizens of the Copper Basin,
and Stan (always).

The copper bosses killed you Joe

They shot you Joe said I;

Takes more than guns to kill a man,

Said Joe I did not die.

Joe Hill ain't dead he says to me,

Joe Hill ain't never died:

Where working men are out on strike,

Joe Hill is at their side.

—excerpt from "I Dreamed I Saw Joe Hill Last Night"
Written by Alfred Hayes, published 1934
Sung by Joan Baez at Woodstock, 1969

CHAPTER 1
Bridges

Living in Coppertown was like living on the moon. The whole area was raw ground, bare and bumpy from erosion ditches cuttin' through every which way. As far as the horizon, it looked like a wrinkled, brown paper bag. There weren't any bushes, nor grass neither—no green things weaving through to settle our homes into the land and make 'em look like they belonged. So why did Miss Post bother teaching us about trees when we didn't have any?

Miners used 'em all up when they started mining copper here a hundred years ago. They cut down the trees to feed the open smelting heaps where they roasted the ore. The smoke from those stacks made acid rain, which killed off everything else. They don't do it that way no more, but nature never did come back.

Even so, Miss Post said we should all know what a tulip poplar, the Tennessee state tree, looked like, and be able to tell it apart from a pine, oak, sassafras, or maple. She said it wasn't normal to not have trees, though it seemed normal to us.

She showed us slide after slide of trees on the pull-down projection screen—thick brown trunks with leafy green tops, or long, slender branches with brushlike needles. She might as well have been showing us spaceships for all that we knew about 'em. Outside our classroom window, all we saw was what the locals called the Red Hills—land that was only good for mining copper and riding BMX bicycles.

Not that I had one.

My first bike was cheap and got busted up from me zooming down dirt roads and jumping erosion ditches—catching air, like a bird in flight. I'd had it since I was ten, so it was too small for me anyhow. I kept hinting to Mom that I needed the real deal for Christmas, a new BMX racer like the one in the Company store window. But she kept saying it was too expensive and dangerous, which made no sense at all. If I'd had a bike, after all, I wouldn't a been *walking* with Piran that day back in August when we ran into Eli and his friends, and I might not have broken my arm.

Bein' named after the patron saint of tin mining, you'd think my best friend would be some sort of angel. But he got us into more trouble than the devil himself. It was his fault I crossed the trestle bridge—I wouldn't a done it if he hadn't dared me.

It was still the hot days of summer then, when the air sat heavy and everything looked sort of golden. Eli Munroe and his gang, a bunch of high-school boys, were hanging out smoking at the end of the trestle bridge when we hiked by on our way to the Old Number 2 Tailings Pond.

"Look at the sweet babies," they said, and laughed. "Bet yu'uns is too chicken to cross the bridge."

"Gimme a break." I rolled my eyes and kept walking, but Piran grabbed my arm.

"C'mon, Jack, let's do it," he said. His face warped through the edge of his thick glasses as he looked at me sideways.

"No way!"

"We'll be in high school after next year, and some of those guys are gonna be seniors then. You want them callin' you coward? Best to prove up now," Piran whispered. "I dare you. I'll even go first."

Piran didn't wait for an answer. He stuck out his chin and stepped onto a railroad tie. Eli and his gang whooped and cheered. I worried Piran's asthma would kick in like it usually did when he was scared or stressed out, but he stayed cool as a cucumber as he balanced from beam to beam. He made it all the way across, jumped to the ground, and turned back to face me with a wide grin.

My turn.

Sunlight reflected off the windshield of Eli's old jacked-up Jeep, and I shaded my eyes. It wasn't the tallest trestle bridge in Polk County, but it was tall enough. At its base, amber water had nearly dried up from the last rain, leaving a yellow mud thick around the bridge's tarred beams. From end to end, it was probably no farther than running from first to second base, but I'd never run on beams spaced too close together for normal steps and so high off the ground.

Down in the basin, even though we didn't have trees, the hills that surrounded us hid things well enough. I listened for the train, but it was quiet—Coppertown quiet—no bugs or birds. No wind neither, which made me sweat all the more.

There was no way out of it. If I didn't cross, not only would I never live it down with the likes of Eli, but Piran would probably never speak to me again.

I took a deep breath, rubbed the lucky rabbit's foot in my pocket, and followed.

I was only halfway across the bridge when the train *chug, chug, chugged* into view.

"Run, RUN!" everybody hollered. But there was no way I could make it to the other side in time, and it was too far down to jump. The railroad ties stuck out like hangers beyond the tracks, which gave me an idea. I kneeled down and crawled to the edge, splinters burying themselves in my hands and knees. I gritted my teeth and grunted through the pain. The train drew closer as I wrapped my arms around one of those hangers and let my legs swing over the side.

For a moment I kicked, my feet seeking purchase on something, anything. But all they hit was air. My stomach turned upside down and my head spun. I pressed my cheek against the hot, sticky tar on the beam as I held on. It stunk like burning tires up so close.

Stay away from Company property, Jack, I remembered my dad saying. *It's dangerous.* But the Company owned nearly everything around and there wasn't much left to do in Coppertown without some sort of danger involved. What was I supposed to do, stay inside all summer? I was old enough to take care of myself. Still, right then I was wishin' I'd listened.

The train roared toward me, its whistle shrieking so loud my head rang. From where I hung barely below its path, it looked like an enormous iron monster with a front grill full of metal teeth rushin' to chew me up— fierce and hungry.

I couldn't feel my fingers anymore, let alone the rest of me. Later, I claimed the vibrations shook me loose— but to tell the God's honest truth, I let go.

I dropped a hundred feet into the mud below. Okay, maybe it was just fifteen feet, but I remember the *squish!* and *splat!* of all that mud, which probably saved my life, right before the *crack!*

Pain shot through my arm.

Eli and his gang couldn't get out of there fast enough. They climbed over each other, piling into his beat-up old Jeep, and took off in a cloud of dust. But one of 'em was slow and got left behind.

"Will McCaffrey!" Piran shouted. "That's Ray Hicks's son in that ditch and yer dad works at the mine. Do I need to spell out what'll happen if you don't get help, and fast?"

I didn't know whether to hate Piran or love him at that moment, but I didn't have much time to think about it. I blacked out.

When I came to, Piran was sitting next to me sucking on his inhaler and crying about how sorry he was for gettin' me into that fix. I was crying because I hurt so bad. He wedged himself underneath me so his leg was a pillow for my head. It was awkward, but we were such a blubbering mess, I didn't care. When the tears dried up and Piran's breathing calmed down, he told me jokes to keep my mind off the pain I was in.

Of course, I'd already heard all his jokes before.

"Don't you have any new material?" I gasped.

"Dang, I don't know. I'm sorry, Jack." Piran teared up again. "My pa is gonna kill me when he hears about this—especially that we was headin' to the old tailings pond…"

We weren't supposed to be there either. It was where the Company dumped water they used for separating out the last of the minerals from the ore. When they closed a pond, they'd stop pumpin' water into it. So, despite the name, the Old Number 2 Tailings Pond didn't look like a pond at all. It was all dried up, with nothing but white, crusty silicate dust in its place, which blew all over Coppertown on windy days. The tailings pond looked like a desert with copper-colored water seepin' around the edges and covering rocks in mustard-colored iron slime. The acres and acres of the tailings pond looked even more barren than the rest of Coppertown, which is why we thought it was cool, I guess. It looked like another planet, so we pretended we were on *Star Trek* out there and zapped each other with invisible ray guns.

"You don't have to tell him," I choked out.

"Why else would we be out this far? My dad may not be a miner, but he's not stupid."

"Heck, he might be the smartest of 'em all," I struggled to say. The sun beat down on us like an oven. I was so thirsty, my tongue swelled to baseball-size. "He doesn't have to go underground for his job." Piran's dad was the town's postmaster. It seemed like it embarrassed him sometimes.

"But underground is where the big money is," he said. "If it weren't for my asthma, I'd be a miner."

I had to be hallucinating. "What? Why?"

"Are you kidding?" Piran replied. "It never rains or snows down there, stays the same temperature all year. The whole town treats you like royalty and you get a discount at the Company store. I want to be a miner like you someday."

Like me? I tried to swallow, but my throat was too dry.

I wanted to love mining like Piran did, like my dad did—the hard hats, the strength, the camaraderie. But then I'd think about all the people I knew of who'd been killed or injured in the mines—all the explosions and collapses. How Dad had to scrub at the end of each day but never did come all the way clean.

None of that seemed to scare my dad. His father, my grandfather Hicks, was killed 'fore I was born, and my dad wore his death like a badge of honor.

We're miners, Jack, he'd say. *It's in our blood.*

One thing I was sure of, mining was *not* in *my* blood. Dad was expecting me to follow in his footsteps and I'd have to tell him I didn't want to before long. It made my stomach hurt. He went to work in the mine at seventeen, and his brother, my uncle Amon, at fifteen—just two years older than me.

"Maybe you could put in a good word for me once you get in there," Piran said.

I moaned. Partly to shut him up but mostly because I hurt so bad and the thinking was makin' me hurt even worse.

It took forever for help to come, but it finally did. The paramedics had to carry me out on a stretcher—a space-age, orange skateboard-looking thing. I thought I'd never get out of that ditch with them panting like they'd never climbed a hill in their lives. It was almost a good thing when they nearly dropped me and I blacked out again. It spared me the pain of half the journey up the crumbling, rocky slope.

I was still wearin' the cast when we went back to school in September. Piran made the story bigger and bigger with every retelling until I was positively famous. The whole class signed my arm, including my entire Miners baseball team.

My cousin Buster said, "I would've killed you if you broke it during baseball season."

Like breakin' it over summer vacation was any better? I guess it was Buster's bass-ackward way of saying he cared. Or not.

I stuck a pencil under the edge of my cast and tried to scratch an itch that was…just out of reach. I could hardly wait to get the danged thing off.

"Jack Hicks, are you paying attention?" Miss Post snapped. "What is special about this tree?" she asked as she pointed her yardstick at the projection screen and another bushy-topped tree.

"It's green?" I said, and everybody laughed. But I thought it was a good answer. In my world of brown earth, yellow mud, and dirty arm casts, anything green seemed special to me. In fact, I'd have turned all of Coppertown green if I could.

CHAPTER 2
Roof Fall

nybody else? What are trees good for?" Miss Post asked.

"Climbin'?" Piran said. It was the all-American-boy pastime, according to the TV shows we watched. Although, I knew for a fact Piran had never climbed a tree in his life.

"Shade," Buster mumbled like it was obvious. But shade was something we didn't get much of around here.

"Yes, good!" Miss Post jumped on his response since Buster rarely said anything in class. She switched to the next slide. It was a diagram, a cutaway view of the ground with rainwater digging in and forming deep crevices. "And their roots hold the soil in place. Without roots, you get erosion like what we have in Coppertown—"

Suddenly, a sharp whirring sound cut her off. *Siren!*

Books flew. Chairs fell. Desks crashed against each other. We took off running straight down Water Street to the Company—all of us. Miss Post couldn't a stopped us if she tried. Our legs just took over.

The Company siren meant something bad had happened in the mine. Somebody's dad might be hurt, or worse.

Please not my dad, please not my dad, I chanted as my feet pounded the road, matching my heartbeat. The sound of rushing blood filled my ears and drowned out the gasping breaths of my classmates as I struggled to race to the front. I squinted at the gray and windy sky—a storm was coming and I was living my nightmare. No matter how fast I ran, I couldn't run fast enough.

Over a rise, the Company came into view like a black scab on the horizon. Its rusted metal pipes wove up, down, over, and through each other like a giant tangle of snakes. The red-and-white-striped smokestack soared out of the center. The whole structure of small buildings and sulfuric acid tanks sat on its own mountain of slag— the leftover molten rock they poured down the hillside. It cooled to a rusty black shade, the same color as the iron train, *the* train, the same train from the trestle bridge incident, which sat waiting for its next shipment at the bottom of the hill. In the yard, in front of the elevator lift, I could already see the commotion.

Piran caught up with me as we slammed against the chain-link fence that surrounded the plant. He gasped large breaths and nodded my way. I glanced at the sign hanging next to the gate: "No copper mine injuries in 28 days. Let's make 1986 our safest year!"

Had that number ever gone over thirty?

Inside the chain-link fence that surrounded the Company, the ambulance's back end faced the elevator lift with its doors open wide. Two men rushed out of the ambulance holding a stretcher, just like the one they'd carried me on. Heck, it mighta been the same one. I gulped.

The paramedics squeezed into the small metal box and we watched the tops of their heads disappear as they sank into the mine shaft. The truck's flashing lights burned spots on my eyes as I stared at the miners, trying to make out what was going on.

What was it this time—roof fall, cave-in, explosion?

Suddenly, a white Ford sped through the gate and skidded to a stop beside the ambulance. I knew that car. Aunt Catherine jumped out and pushed her way to the lift as the wind whipped her hair over her face.

My stomach tied in a knot and I tore away from my classmates to run inside the gate. Instead, I hit the wide chest of a soot-covered miner. He was dressed in dark denim overalls, with a flannel shirt and a hard hat. He smelled of sweat and sulfur, bitter, like scratched metal. It made my teeth ache. "Yu'uns best stay outside the fence," he said in a gruff voice.

"But that's my aunt!" I shouted. "It must be Uncle Amon! What happened to my uncle?"

"Amon Hicks? Don't know yet." He looked at me closer. "You Ray Hicks's son?"

"I'm Jack," I croaked and nodded. I couldn't catch my breath.

He stepped aside and I ran to Aunt Catherine. She looked at me like a scared rabbit and my first instinct was to run away, but she hugged me hard, bending my cast against my body at a strange angle. It pinched and I inhaled from the sharp pain, but I didn't say nothin'.

The yard grew quiet as everybody stopped and waited.

Aunt Catherine and I sat on the hood of her car until the engine cooled and grew metal cold. She rocked back and forth, twisting the ring on her finger. She and Amon had only been married a year.

I couldn't think of anything to say to make her feel better, so I just kept my mouth shut, even when her hair whipped around from the wind and stung my cheeks.

A miner handed her a cup of coffee and she passed it to me, but I didn't want it either. I didn't mind the taste, but the few times I'd drunk coffee it had torn my stomach up worse than usual, so I didn't care for it. Besides, it seemed too calm a thing to do—sip a drink— when who knows what was going on a hundred feet below us. I wanted to throw the cup across the yard and shout, *Hurry up already!* But there was nothin' to do but wait.

I poured the dark liquid out next to the tire, where it stained the gravel like blood.

After what was probably an hour, the lift chugged back into motion. It was coming up. Finally. And yet, now that it was happening I decided I could wait a while longer—maybe forever if it meant avoiding bad news.

The metal gates pushed open with a *clang*. Folks outside the gate rushed in and everybody started shouting, "Out of the way! Give 'em room!"

Aunt Catherine ran to the stretcher and grabbed the hand that lay limp over its side. Uncle Amon's hand— dirty and…gray.

The crowd swallowed me up as I stood there, frozen.

"It's Amon Hicks," whispered around me like a Sunday prayer.

The paramedics loaded my uncle into the ambulance and my aunt climbed in with him. Suddenly my dad was there too, covered in more dirt and grime than I'd ever seen on him.

"Not enough room," the paramedics yelled to him.

"I'll meet you at the hospital, Amon. You're gonna be okay!" Dad shouted. He stumbled to his Company truck as if he couldn't see his way clearly, as if his world was rocking beneath him.

I waved my good arm and chased after him to pick me up. "Dad, Dad!" But he didn't notice. My eyes stung with angry tears as Piran grabbed my arm.

"C'mon!"

We took off running again—this time cross-country toward the hospital. Up and down through the erosion ditches we climbed and slid. The wind kicked up dirt devils that blew into my eyes and nose, but going that way was faster than the road.

Piran couldn't make it. About halfway there, his asthma stopped him flat. "Go on," he choked out as he bent over coughing. "I'll catch up."

"But, but..." I stammered. I was used to waiting for him to catch his breath.

"I'll be fine!" He wheezed and pulled his inhaler from his pocket, wiggling it as if to say, *See, I didn't forget it this time.* "Go!"

I nodded and kept runnin'.

My arm throbbed under its cast as I burst through the emergency room doors. The waiting room was already full of miners and their families—word traveled fast in our town.

Aunt Livvy, Uncle Bubba, and Buster stood near the check-in desk with my mom, whose eyes were filled with tears. She reached out a shaky hand and pulled me close.

Suddenly, a gut-wrenching scream echoed from deep inside the building. All the air left the room in one gasp as everybody faced the silver double doors. A short time later, the doctor pushed through, scanned the crowd, and then shook his head. "I'm sorry, there was nothing we could do."

I tried to swallow back the pressure growing inside—I didn't want Buster to see me that way—but it didn't work. I was crying for real now. We all were. My tears joined in with the groans, wails, and cursing that spread through the room. Mom hugged me tight, and though I usually would have pulled away, I didn't complain when the buttons of her shirt pressed into my forehead and her tears melted into my hair.

Aunt Catherine's parents frantically wrestled their way through the crowd. "Catherine! Where's our Catherine?" Mrs. Maddox shouted.

Just then Dad appeared through the silver doors. "She's with Amon," he mumbled and held a door open for them. As soon as they passed through, he fell into Mom's arms and sobbed.

I'd never seen my dad cry, and it dried up my own tears real quick. He'd lost his dad and now his brother to the mine. How could he stand it? Mom held him close, just like she'd held me, as she rubbed his back and whispered, "It'll be okay. It'll be okay."

"I told him to stop sometimes, to listen to the rock," Dad said. His face was puffy, streaked with dirt and tears. "If only I'd been there. He probably didn't even notice the roof was givin' way..."

Roof fall then. It was always something like that. And now my uncle Amon was dead.

Three days later I stood between Mom and Grandpa Chase by Uncle Amon's grave. Dad and Aunt Catherine stood on either side of Father Huckabay, our Episcopal minister. The rest of the town surrounded us. Grandpa pointed out the Union leaders who drove in from the big city. They stood toward the back, away from the crowd with Sheriff Elder.

Everybody wore black, but dirt whipped around our ankles and turned us red up to our knees. I looked down at my own big feet, which seemed to melt right into the ground. Mom squeezed my hand and my eyes watered up again.

It had been a closed casket at the wake the night before—it gave me shivers to think why. But it felt strange that I didn't get to say goodbye, or somethin'. Amon and my dad never did get along real well. They'd been in the middle of another row when the accident happened, so it had been a few weeks since I'd seen Amon…alive.

They lowered the casket into what looked like a small sinkhole in the red earth—much like the collapse where Grandfather Hicks had died. Was I the only one who thought it strange? It was being underground that killed Uncle Amon, and here we were puttin' him right back under.

After it was done, Aunt Catherine went to stay with her sister out of town. She said she couldn't stand being around Amon's memory everywhere, said she needed a fresh start. I hoped it made losing Amon easier for her, because it sure weren't easy at home. My home.

Dad didn't sleep for days, it seemed. He kept switchin' between being sad and mad at Amon. According to him, Amon never should have been down there in the first place.

After Grandfather Hicks had been killed in that collapse way back when, my dad had gone to work in the mines to keep the family going. His mother had insisted Amon stay in school. She said both her boys weren't gonna lose out on a chance at a better life. After she died a few months later from a broken heart, Amon quit school and went to work in the mines anyway. The money was too good, I guess.

If it had been me, I wouldn't have done what Amon did. I would have stayed in school and studied. I don't know what I would have studied—something, anything to keep me out of those mines.

But Dad had my future mapped out for me. I was supposed to be a miner too. Would Amon's dying change his mind? Maybe Dad wouldn't want me to be a miner anymore. Maybe *he* wouldn't want to be a miner anymore.

It could have easily been him killed in the roof fall. In my dreams that gray hand hanging over the side of the stretcher didn't belong to my uncle Amon. It belonged to my dad.

CHAPTER 3
Castoffs

Two weeks later, I awoke to the sound of Dad's Company truck engine turnin' over. His new tires, the third set so far this year from the acid eating 'em up, crunched over the gravely dirt yard. I sat up in bed, groggy, and watched out the window as he drove across the bridge.

Usually I could watch him drive all the way to the Company, but today he disappeared into thick fog.

I rubbed my lucky rabbit's foot and tried to settle my stomach as I prayed like I did every day. *Please let him come home safe, please let him come home safe.* I knew it was silly, but I'd been chanting that prayer since I was a little kid. It made me feel like I was doing *something* to help my dad. Maybe if I'd been doing it for my uncle too... I added a prayer for all the other miners.

I got my lucky rabbit's foot when I was eight and went to Rock City in Chattanooga with my grandpa and grandma Chase, before she died of lung cancer. There were so many signs to "See Rock City" painted on barn roofs along the way, I couldn't wait to hike through the caves with their crystal-lined walls and diorama scenes of fairy tales and gnomes at work tucked into nooks and crannies. I wanted to wind through the "Fat Man's Squeeze," a path between two rock faces, and see seven states from the overlook.

It wasn't until I was older that I realized how strange it was that Grandpa had wanted to go into caves for his vacation after a lifetime of mining. After all, he'd been in the same mine collapse that killed Grandfather Hicks.

They were best friends when it happened. Grandpa Chase made it out with a back injury and couldn't mine anymore, which is why he opened the Bait 'n Beer, but my dad's father didn't make it out at all. Grandpa Chase said he didn't miss the mining, but he did miss being underground. Despite the bad things that had happened, he said it was like being in the womb of Mother Nature.

If I'd felt that way about being underground, it woulda made things easier with my dad. Even as far back as that trip to Rock City, I knew my heart was someplace else.

It was one of my first trips out of Coppertown and I'd never seen so much green. I couldn't stop gaping at all the trees that towered over our car. It was so seldom I had to look *up* to see anything in Coppertown, other than the sky. When I finally saw the caves, I couldn't have cared less—I'd seen plenty of rocks in my lifetime. What I fell in love with were the trees.

I rubbed my lucky rabbit's foot and remembered standing outside Rock City, under the shadow of a tree— Grandma had called it a maple—and having to crane my neck all the way back and strain to see the top through a thick canopy of paper-thin leaves. They looked like stained glass as the light cut through their layers in a million shades of green. I'd placed my hand on the trunk to brace myself and swore I could feel it hum. I felt like I was in church—experiencing something holy, like the tree was talking to me somehow.

About a month after that trip, I found a poster of trees, just trees, in *National Geographic* magazine and I put it up on my bedroom wall. Sometimes I dreamed I was a bird flying above that thick forest, breathing in all that *green*.

Dad loved everything underground, and I guess

Grandpa Chase did too, but I loved everything above. Well, everything that was *supposed* to be above anyhow.

The poster reminded me of what Miss Post had said on the day Uncle Amon died. Tree roots hold the soil together. But we didn't have any trees in Coppertown. If we did, would Uncle Amon still be alive? Could trees somehow save my dad?

How long would it take to grow a forest?

I imagined seedlings sproutin' and spreading their roots underground while up top they reached toward the sun, at first no larger than twigs, then with trunks growing wider and taller. Their branches stretched every which way, leaves popping out along them in green waves. They made shadows across our Red Hills, where no shadows had fallen before. The air cooled, birds nested, and me and Piran climbed tree limbs higher and higher, breathing deeply without any dust in our lungs.

Even in my imaginings, though, a forest took a long time. And considerin' we could never get anything to grow in Mom's garden, let alone anywhere else in Coppertown, it would be longer still. I sighed.

Then I remembered what day it was—Friday. Not only was it the last day before the weekend, but my arm cast was coming off. Finally!

I got out of bed and dressed in record time. The smell of sausage frying up in the iron skillet wrapped around me as I walked down the hall. My stomach growled.

"Biscuits and gravy for breakfast," Mom said. "Pour yourself some milk."

"No eggs?" I could've eaten the eggs and the chicken too.

"I gave your dad the last one. I'll pick up some from the Company store later today." She looked out the window. "It's foggy this morning. Can't do laundry." She sighed. "The fog ate up my stockings last time and I can't keep buying a new pair every time I need to wear 'em."

Our fog was like sticky acid rain, and it burned holes in Mom's stockings in a matter of hours. "I closed my bedroom window," I said. It kept the wet out.

"Good. I hope it doesn't get as hot today, though," she said. "Law' me, it gets stuffy in here all shut up tight."

She started singing "As the Sparrow Goes" by Anita Carter. She'd been singing that tune since I don't know when. I don't think she even noticed she was doing it. Like a bird, she yodeled, "As the sparrow flies, my heart flies, bringing my love to you." It was the sound of my mother.

I stuffed myself silly with two biscuits smothered in gravy.

"Jack, you're gonna choke yourself. Slow down," Mom said.

"In my opinion, biscuits are the world's most perfect food," I said with a grin. It took an entire glass of milk to wash that brick down to the bottom of my stomach, where it sat warm and happy.

Mom handed me my lunch in a brown paper sack. "Now remember, I'll pick you up after lunch and we'll head to the hospital."

It had to be the only time in history those words had ever sounded good. "I won't forget!"

"Kiss." She tapped her cheek as I was about to leave.

"Awww, Mom. I'm gettin' too old for all that mush."

She grabbed my face and planted a kiss on my forehead.

"You are never too old to love on your mama."

For days after Uncle Amon died, the kids at school had avoided me like I was stained with bad luck or something. They'd stare and stop talking whenever I was near. But today they weren't—maybe because I couldn't stop smiling.

"Will you quit it?" Piran said as we walked down the hall. "Everybody is lookin' at you."

"I can't help it," I said as I nearly danced out of my worn sneakers. "I'm getting my cast off after lunch!"

"Well, that's good." Piran's ears turned red, a sure sign he still felt bad about it. "But maybe you could stop *bouncing* so much? You're makin' a scene."

"Hey, at least they're not whisperin' anymore," I said and my stomach relaxed a little.

I had a hard time focusing on the tree identification quiz, so I only got an A minus. Piran got a C, which he was pretty happy with.

"It's impossible to study at my house," he said. If I was around Piran's older sister, Hannah, all the time, I wouldn't have been able to study either. But it wasn't Hannah he was talking about. "My sisters and brothers are always runnin' around screaming," he added. I'd seen and heard it too many times to doubt him—the volume got louder there every year. Dad said Mrs. Quinn spit out babies like a Pez dispenser.

Once, I asked Mom why I didn't have any brothers or sisters. She said they'd tried two times before me, but lost 'em both. The way she teared up, I decided not to ask any more questions about it. I liked thinking I had a brother and sister up in heaven somewhere, though. Add them to Grandfather and Grandmother Hicks, Grandma Chase, and Uncle Amon, and I had an army of guardian angels up there lookin' out for me.

As promised, Mom was at school after lunch, her car kicking up a cloud of dirt as it pulled up to the front steps. I didn't want dust in my teeth so while I waited for the cloud to settle before I got in, I yelled to my cousin who was still playin' catch in the yard. "Hey, Buster, next time I see you I'll be able to play ball!"

"'Bout danged time!" he shouted and fake pitched the ball at me. I ducked and he laughed. But he mighta really done it. I wouldn't have put it past him.

Talking about removing my cast and doin' it were two different things, though. We had to go back to the same place where Uncle Amon died just two weeks before. Walking into the hospital's waiting room brought that afternoon back like a bad dream. I could almost hear Aunt Catherine's scream still echoing off the seafoam-green walls—the color of my least favorite crayon. When we'd seen Aunt Catherine's parents in town a couple days before, they'd said they didn't know when she'd be back from visiting her sister, their faces tightening up like they were wondering if she ever would come home.

My arm tickled like it knew something was up and my feet wanted to head the other way. I tried not to fidget while we waited for the nurse to call my name. I watched the clock *tick, tick, tick* and stared at the walls. Who decided that sea-foam green was a calming color anyhow? It made me nauseous.

"Jack Hicks?" the nurse said. It was time.

She led us back through the two large silver doors to a row of beds divided by curtains hanging from the ceiling.

"Go ahead and get yourself settled," she said and patted a bed. "Dr. Davis will be with you in a minute."

Dr. Davis had been my doctor since I was born. Mom said he moved to Coppertown straight out of medical school and never left. Something about our town got under people's skin, in a good way. Didn't surprise me none—we were full of good people. Although if we had trees, I bet even more folks would stick around.

I climbed onto the high bed, crunching the white paper underneath me and feeling all of five years old. *Was this the same bed my uncle died on?* My insides jumped like oil in a hot skillet, though I was tryin' my best to stay calm.

In, out, in, out. I closed my eyes and breathed. *My stomach is fine. I don't feel sick.* Then Dr. Davis showed up and plugged in his saw.

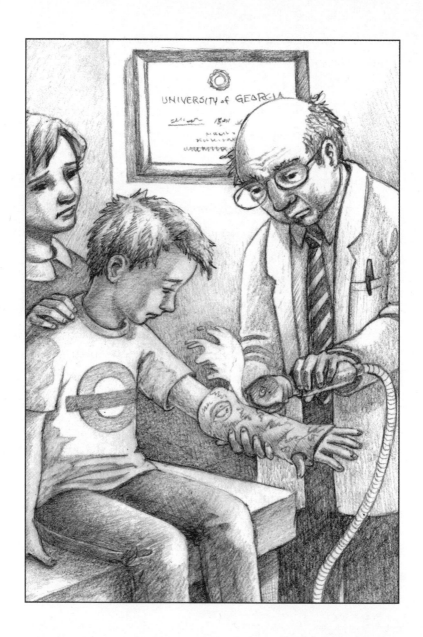

I don't know if I was curious or just plum scared, but I had to watch as the blade spun toward my arm. The high-pitched scream filled the small room and bounced off the cement block walls. I flinched to cover my ears, but Dr. Davis said, "Jack, hold still now. This'll only take a minute."

Plaster dust sprayed up like a rooster tail as the saw sank into my cast. I ignored the dust flying and stared without blinking while Dr. Davis moved the blade up and down my arm, cutting deeper and deeper until the tension of the cast released. The blade moved dangerously close to my pale skin as he cut the last bits of fiber that still held. Finally, the cast popped apart. My flattened arm hairs tried to stand on end as air rushed around them for the first time in weeks.

"See, that wasn't so bad, was it?" Dr. Davis asked as he wrestled the cast completely off.

"I don't feel so good," I said.

"Oh, you'll be fine." He patted my leg and handed me a yellow sucker.

Then I puked all over his white coat.

"Stop lookin' at it," Mom said in the car. "I don't need you throwing up again."

"It looks so weird."

The broken arm was skinnier than my other arm and felt much lighter. Except for the red spots where I'd scratched under the cast with a bottle brush, it was strangely pale. Even with the cast gone, it still itched like wildfire.

"Jack Hicks!" Mom swatted at my hand. "Stop scratching."

"It makes it feel better."

"You won't have any skin left if you don't cut it out. Anyhow, look in the back seat. I got you a present."

"A bike?" I smiled.

"No, not a bike." She rolled her eyes. "Good Lord, don't you think you get in enough trouble without wheels added to the mix?"

"If I'd had a bike, I'd a been going too fast past the trestle bridge to even notice Eli and all them that day." I reached over the seat and grabbed the box from the back.

"You shouldn't a been going to the tailings pond in the first place, young man—it's dangerous out there."

"I know, I know." I didn't get grounded for it because of my broken arm, and I didn't want Mom to remember that, so I opened the lid quickly. "Converse high-tops, cool!" It wasn't a BMX bike, but Converse weren't bad. "Thanks, Mom."

"Well, maybe these will keep *your feet* and you out of trouble—at least for a little while, please?"

"Yes, ma'am." I blushed and hoped she was only kidding about the bike. She'd been grinnin' when she said it, so it could still happen.

The Randy Travis song Mom had been humming along to was replaced by a deep voice that sounded strangely familiar.

"Is that Bo Duke from *The Dukes of Hazzard*?" I asked and scrunched up my face.

"You don't like it?"

"He shoulda stuck with TV," I said and tried to block out the sappy love song.

The Dukes of Hazzard was my favorite TV show. I watched the reruns all the time. It was about two former moonshine runners who were staying on the right side of the law now but still got in trouble with the sheriff all the time anyhow.

Moonshine used to be a big thing up in these hills. Back during the Prohibition era when alcohol was illegal, folks would make moonshine and then outrun the cops trying to get it to the big cities to sell. It's how a lot of mountain folks made a living during hard times. When alcohol became legal again, it put a lot of families out of business.

The show took place in what was supposed to be today's time in the Appalachian Mountains, but the accents were too thick and it was sort of cheesy. Bo and Luke Duke's clashes with the sheriff led to lots of car chases, though, which is why I liked it. Before my old bike fell apart, Piran and I used to pretend we were Bo and Luke Duke, racing around the erosion ditches like we were driving the General Lee, their 1969 Dodge Charger. That was my dream car.

I looked out the window, but the bright sun hit the glass just so and I ended up staring at my own reflection. Shadows stood out under my nose and eyebrows, and I squished up my face to turn them into odd shapes. It would have worked better if I had strong, sharp edges like my dad, but I had my mom's roundness along with her olive skin, brown hair that would never lie down straight, and dark eyes.

Mom said my coloring came from a Cherokee ancestor. This used to be Cherokee land. Sometimes Piran and I found arrowheads or pieces of pottery lyin' around.

Most Native Americans were forced away on the Trail of Tears, but some hid out in the mountains and slowly blended back into society. Grandpa Chase told me, "You can't swing a dead cat without hittin' Indian blood in Coppertown." I liked the idea of being part Indian. They never would have stripped the land the way the Company had. They lived *with* nature. It made me proud to know I had that in me too.

As we drove past the Company, I squinted through my reflection at the red-and-white-striped smokestack that marked its location from miles away. Without trees, it was the tallest thing in these parts. Heck, it'd probably be the tallest thing even with trees. You could never get lost in Coppertown as long as you could see the smokestack.

Coote Epworth walked alongside the road near the entrance to the mine, mumbling to himself as he always did. Crazy Coote, as folks called him, was bent and skinny with a stubbly beard. He always wore either a blue, green, or red hooded sweatshirt with worn blue jeans and kept his hands stuffed deep in his pockets.

"Coote's wearing red today"—or "green" or "blue"— we'd say when we saw him. He was kind of our town mascot, even though he was nuts.

"Mom, why does he just walk around all the time?"

I turned in my seat to watch him out the back window. *And what's he saying?*

"You remember hearing about that big mine collapse way back when, before you were born?"

"The one Grandfather Hicks died in?"

"No, the other one, from when they got too close to another mine shaft robbing the drifts for ore. Your grandfather warned they shouldn't do it, but management told 'em to anyway. They said it was insured, so they should try. Well, the explosion made the mine unstable," Mom said. "Coote's mama was pregnant when his daddy was killed in it. She took to drinking and Coote came out a little funny. The insurance money didn't matter then."

I frowned and promised myself I wouldn't make fun of Coote anymore.

We stopped at the gas station on the way home. Mom was just pulling up to the full-service side as usual when none other than Eli Munroe came rushin' out in greasy overalls with Mr. Habersham right on his heels snapping a gray towel like a whip. "And don't you ever come back, you stupid kid!"

Eli jumped into his worn-out Jeep and peeled out of the lot, glancing at me with a scowl as he veered into traffic. Several cars swerved to avoid being hit.

"Sorry you had to see that, Mrs. Hicks. Kid was smoking a cigarette right next to an oil drum. 'Bout blew us up. He's as sharp as a butter knife, that one." Mr. Habersham rubbed the dirty rag over his red face, which didn't help matters. "Fill you up?"

"Regular, please," Mom said and handed him her Exxon card.

"Why isn't he in school?" I wondered out loud.

"Didn't he graduate last year?" Mom asked.

"No, he's supposed to be a senior," I said.

She shook her head. "Shame."

At home, I placed the cast next to my baseball trophies on the shelf under my bedroom window. In a way, it was a trophy too. I smiled at all the signatures. They were so different. Some were loopy, some were scratchy. Sonny Rust, the Company manager's son, had drawn a smiley face like John Hancock's big signature on the Declaration of Independence. He was always trying too hard to fit in. At least the smiley face was on the underside where it wasn't starin' at me.

I changed my clothes, putting on a fresh pair of jeans and a plaid flannel shirt from the bureau, since the ones I'd had on were covered with plaster dust. It was so nice to pull my shirt on without a cast. I wiggled my fingers as they poked out the end of my sleeve. Then I leaned over and tied up my new sneakers.

Piran will be jealous. I frowned. I wished I could buy him a pair too.

Piran didn't get new things very often and when he did, it was usually something "practical." His family wasn't poor or anything, but the postmaster's job didn't pay nearly as good as mining, so money had to stretch in their house.

"Jack, dinner," Mom called from the kitchen. "I made your favorite, macaroni and cheese."

"Let's see that arm," Dad said as I ran into the kitchen. I held it out for him to inspect. "It looks kinda puny."

"Don't worry. You'll build it back up in no time."

"We saw that Munroe boy at the gas station today," Mom said as she set a large dish of yellow globby goodness on the table. "Mr. Habersham fired him for smokin' near an oil drum."

"I'm not surprised," Dad said. "He applied for a job at the mine last week, but that boy is about as bright as a coon-oil lantern on a foggy day. He wouldn't last a week underground."

Dad got quiet and cleared his throat. It seemed that everything reminded him of Amon, which turned his mood to dark clouds as quick as spit. He reached for the serving spoon and plopped two huge helpings of macaroni and cheese onto his plate like he was angry at it.

Save some for me, I worried.

"Jack, do you know you'll be a seventh-generation copper miner?" he said.

Of course I knew. Like most of our neighbors, we even hung the flag of Cornwall, England, below our American flag—black with a white cross representing the tin that ran through the ground there.

"And there's no telling how long our family was mining tin in England before we came to America," he continued.

"Ray, stop," Mom whispered. "Not during dinner."

"What about Uncle Amon?" I gulped.

"He weren't no miner," he mumbled and the muscles in his face sank like melting snow. "He never should have been down there to begin with. Mama didn't want him to... It's why I wouldn't hire Eli. It's a team down there. Those men gotta be able to trust you. One man not paying attention to what the rock is sayin' puts everybody in danger." He pointed his fork at me. "But don't you worry, Jack. You're my son. You're made of the right stuff and you'll make a damned fine miner."

"Ray, will you just stop?" Mom glared at him until he sighed and went back to his dinner.

I knew I should have been flattered by what he said. He'd dropped out of high school to take care of his family when Grandfather Hicks died in the collapse and had moved up quickly, despite never getting his high school diploma.

"Hard work will get you anywhere," he'd say.

But he never bothered to ask me what I wanted to do, which was pretty much anything other than mining. *Do you even care what I think?* I wanted to yell. Did it matter to him? But how could I tell my dad that I didn't want his life?

I couldn't move my fork. Who knew you could get a stomachache from macaroni and cheese?

Mom looked at me with her forehead all wrinkled. "Eat up, Jack. We've got to get goin' to the park."

I couldn't hold on to my bad mood for music night— Hannah would be there!

CHAPTER 4

Music Night

F riday night was music night. Being the last one of the season, nearly everybody in town would gather at the river park in Georgia for bluegrass.

Coppertown sat right at the intersection of Polk County in Tennessee and Fannin County in Georgia. Cherokee County in North Carolina was just a stone's throw away too. In fact, the Tennessee-Georgia state line ran right through the parking lot of the Company store.

Piran and I had stood with a foot in each state many a time. It made me feel like I'd been around, which I hadn't.

We caught up with Grandpa Chase as we walked down to the park with our folding chairs. Dad and I helped him unload some coolers from his truck. Since Grandpa owned the local Bait 'n Beer, he sold RC Colas and MoonPies for fifty cents during music nights. Course, he couldn't sell beer over the state line because Fannin was a dry county. And with Sheriff Elder right there, nobody was sneakin' in anything they shouldn't.

Grandpa gave me my cola and MoonPies for free. Sometimes I could wrangle one for Piran too.

I was just grabbing one for the both of us when his sister swooped by with her pack of girlfriends in a cloud of paisley and pink. I stuttered out a weak, "H-h-hi, Hannah."

"Oh, hey, Jack," she said and kept going on by. I focused on setting out a folding chair so nobody would notice my grin. Nothing could keep me down on music night.

The river kept the air cool as the water flowed by the park in a wide curve. People came down out of the hills, some so wrinkled and bent, you'd swear they were at least two hundred years old. And they all brought their instruments with 'em—everywhere you looked there were guitars, banjos, fiddles, basses, mandolins, and dulcimers. Sometimes there were more people making music than listening. For everybody else, it was a good time to catch up on gossip.

When Grandpa Chase wasn't sellin', he was sawing away on his fiddle. Mr. Quinn, Piran's dad, plucked like wildfire on his banjo, clawhammer-style. A few kids

stumbled over their fingering, trying to keep up. Mom sang along to "I'll Fly Away" and "Rosewood Casket"—I caught Dad looking at her with a goofy expression on his face. If anybody could get his mind off the mine, it was her.

Old Counce Taylor harmonized with her in his Celtic mountain drawl. When he sang "Angel Band," he blended all the words together until it was nearly impossible to tell what the words were. Grandpa said he sounded like a bagpipe—that it was the old mountain way of singin'.

Aunt Livvy and Uncle Bubba danced a few reels. They were so good people said they could win awards. Buster just grumbled, "God, they're at it again," and tried not to stand too close.

Practically the whole town was there—the miners and the folks whose businesses existed because of the miners. The store owners, the doctors, the service folks, and even Miss Post, who looked pretty in a green dress with her hair down. A man was standing beside her who I didn't recognize. Was he her boyfriend? Did teachers have boyfriends?

At any rate, all the folks from Coppertown were there. We were one big family.

Except for the Rusts, that is. Not only were they from

some big city, Nashville or somewhere, but Mr. Rust was the Company manager. He held the fate of most of our fathers' jobs in his hands.

Since my dad was a supervisor, we'd been invited up to their big Victorian house once. It was over a hundred years old, built by the original owner of the copper mines—I'd never seen anything so fancy. Sonny's bedroom was nearly as big as our kitchen and den combined. And they had a *parlor*—I never could figure out what for—and chandeliers, which were lights with crystals hangin' from the ceiling. I couldn't imagine living in a house like that.

The Rusts were nice enough, I suppose, and tried hard to be a part of our community, but there was no way they ever would. They sat at the edge of the gathering where folks smiled politely to them but didn't ask them to join in.

So other than going to different churches and some folks not getting along with others so well, we were one big family—except for the Rusts. It was kinda like my baseball team, just bigger. I couldn't wait to be playing again, considering I hadn't been able to practice with my cast on. We Miners were as tough as our fathers, undefeated in our region the year before. We planned to do it again the following spring and beat out our biggest rivals, the Rockets.

We lived baseball and would have been playing during music night, but nobody let us practice around all those expensive instruments. We might have let Sonny join in if we had been playing, but since we weren't, Buster, Piran, and I hung out at the water's edge and skipped rocks.

From our position, we could spy the bend in the river where they'd stacked smashed-up cars to keep the bank from eroding. Trees would've done a better job, if there'd been any.

"How's your arm feel without the cast?" Piran asked.

"It aches," I said, the toss of a stone sending shock waves up to my shoulder. "The doc said the bone is set, but it'll still bother me for a while. I'm just glad the cast is gone."

"Me too." The tops of his ears turned pink and he glanced at my feet. "Nice sneakers. Converse?"

"Yeah, Mom got 'em for me." I shrugged and tried not to make a big deal out of it.

"Cool."

As we tossed rock after rock, I tried to watch Hannah out of the corner of my eye. She was a senior and the most beautiful girl in Coppertown—maybe in all the

Appalachians. How she could be related to Piran was beyond me.

Where Piran had wiry hair sticking out the top of his head like popcorn, Hannah's strawberry-blond curls flowed over her freckled shoulders like hot slag pouring down the hillside. Her lips stayed a rosy pink, even though she didn't wear that shiny, banana-smelling lip gloss that the other girls did. And unlike Piran, she got her mom's eyes, crystal blue like the sky on a cloudless day. She didn't play any musical instruments, but oh, could she dance. The setting sun lit her in silhouette as she spun and spun in her pink paisley dress. Time slowed and I...

"No way, Jack. Hannah? She's out of your league, cuz," Buster said and laughed.

I felt heat rise to my cheeks and glanced at Piran, who just rolled his eyes. We were in silent agreement—the less said about my crush, the better. Leave it to Buster to make a scene out of it.

"I bet I can skip this rock six times," Piran said, changing the subject. God bless him.

"I bet I can do seven!" Buster replied, taking the bait.

His disk-shaped rock skipped out across the amber surface of the water, creating small trails of white where it hit. One, two, three, four, five, six... Not seven, but still something to brag about.

It was the kind of night I wished could last forever.

CHAPTER 5
Layoffs

The next week we were into October. Colder weather was finally moving in, and I puffed my breath into doughnut shapes as I walked close to the river. Fog soaked through to my bones. I rubbed my arm.

Piran's head bobbed on his tall, lanky frame as he walked uphill to meet me at the end of the bridge.

"Mornin'," he gasped but didn't pull out his inhaler.

"Mornin'." I waited for him to catch his breath. "Okay?"

Piran walked up Killer Hill almost half a mile to the bridge every day. My walk was only a quarter mile and all downhill. "Yeah. The cold air is just gettin' to me."

"You read that science chapter last night?" I asked.

"I tried to, but I fell asleep." Piran rolled his eyes. "Amphibilans are so boring."

"Amphi*bians*," I said. Along with no trees, we didn't have any frogs or salamanders in Coppertown—there weren't any bugs for them to eat. But I'd put up with bugs if it meant having frogs. "I think they're cool."

"Good. You can tell me all about 'em."

I dove into the details of the frog's life cycle, from egg to tadpole to adult. Piran made snoring noises.

"Fine, fine." I laughed. "But you know you just jinxed yourself. Miss Post will call on you for certain now."

"Eh, I'll study some at lunch."

He didn't, of course.

By noon, the day had warmed up enough for baseball.

Piran pitched and I was at first base. It felt so good to be playing again, even in a loose game of after-lunch baseball, and even if my arm scared me from catchin' anything just yet. It would be too cold and wet to play before too long, so I was anxious to fit in whatever I could.

Standing where we were, Piran and I saw the sulfur cloud first. It was headin' straight toward the ball field.

"Hey yu'uns"—Piran nodded toward the Company— "hold yer breath."

Everybody squinted as the yellow cloud sank onto the field, turning everything a sickly color.

I coughed a few times and felt the familiar burn in my lungs. Sulfur clouds blew through from the Company at least once a week, sometimes more.

Piran reached for his inhaler. We all waited a few minutes to get used to the stink and then went back to playing.

"Hey, Sonny," Buster yelled out, "your dad dealt a mean one that time."

"Ha, ha," Sonny said and looked away. But not before I caught a glimpse of his frown and saw his cheeks turn bright pink.

I kinda felt bad for Sonny sometimes. Nobody really wanted him on the team, but he was a better-than-average shortstop, so we put up with him.

As I predicted, Miss Post called on Piran to answer a question about our amphibians homework.

"How long does it take for a frog to grow from an egg to an adult frog?"

Piran turned white as chalk. I tried to send him

the answer with my brain, but his eyes were big as headlights—nothing was gettin' through.

"Um—" Piran said.

Just then, the classroom door swung open. Principal Slaughter walked straight to the front of the room with a frown etched into his large brow. "Miss Post, I need to speak with you in the hall," he said.

"We're in the middle of a lesson..." Miss Post objected.

"This can't wait," he said and led her out of class.

"Lucky break," I whispered to Piran.

"Yeah," he said and let out the breath he'd obviously been holding.

We straightened up as Miss Post returned. Her face was whiter than Piran's had been.

"Children," she said and took a deep breath, "Principal Slaughter just shared some bad news."

My stomach dropped. The siren wasn't blaring. How bad could it be? Was Dad okay? He could have a broken bone or a concussion, or he might need stitches—those sorts of things happened all the time and the Company didn't run the siren for those.

"The Company is laying people off, a lot of them." She frowned. "Don't worry about the lesson. Go home to your families."

As Piran and I made our way through the school toward the front doors, the sound of sneakers squeaking on linoleum tiles filled the hall instead of the usual laughter. Like astronauts leaving a spaceship, we poured out of the dark building into the glaring sun and joined the growing crowd on Water Street. Nobody was running this time, so we were privy to all the gossip buzzing around us.

"I heard they were laying off a thousand men," Mrs. McCoy said. "That's over half the workforce!"

"That's just a rumor, Ida Mae," Mrs. Abernathy said.

"We'll know soon enough," Mrs. Hill replied.

"My Howard can't lose his job," Mrs. Barnes told everybody. "He's got seniority."

"Doesn't your dad have seniority too?" Piran asked me.

"Yeah, he's worked there forever."

By the time we got to the Company, the first groups of men were already walking past us with their heads down. Their faces looked a lot like Piran's when Miss Post had asked him about the frogs—pale, slack-mouthed, wide-eyed. Their wives rushed to their sides.

"What's that pink paper they're holding?" I asked.

"It's called a pink slip," Mrs. Hill whispered. "It means they don't have a job anymore."

That's when it really hit me. *Layoffs.* For so long,

I'd secretly wished for something to keep Dad out of the mine, to keep him safe. But I'd meant safe from injury. I'd never considered something like this. What would happen if he lost his job?

I'd always imagined "Dad safe" as a sunny picture—I saw him eating pancakes or fiddling around in his metal shop all day. Everybody would be smiling, everybody would be happy. But if Dad lost his job, where would the money come from? How long would it be before we were living in a ramshackle shed like Crazy Coote?

Inside the gate, two men I'd never seen before stood on either side of Mr. Ducat, the Company accountant. Everybody usually liked Mr. Ducat, seeing as he handed out the paychecks, but today they barely looked at him. He waited by the elevator with his box full of envelopes, shifting his weight uncomfortably.

Mr. Rust, Sonny's dad, wasn't anywhere in sight, and neither was Sonny. Go figure.

Everybody got quiet as the hoist whined back into motion to lift another group of men from the mine. When they reached the top, Mr. Ducat riffled through the envelopes and handed them out. Lift after lift, group by group, most of the men were laid off, including Will McCaffrey's dad.

Despite Will being partly responsible for my broken arm, I felt bad for him and his family. What were they gonna do now? There'd been the blue-jeans factory, but it closed two years earlier. Construction might be a good job for a miner, but Coppertown wasn't exactly a booming city. Stores downtown sometimes put out signs when they needed help. I tried to picture a miner dishing out ice cream at Dilbeck's Pharmacy, or taking ticket stubs at the movie theater. It didn't fit. And besides, I hadn't seen a HELP WANTED sign in ages.

My fingers grew numb.

I watched Mr. Barnes open his envelope and pull out a pink slip. His shoulders sagged as he lifted his brass ID tag from the In board and moved it to the Out board, proof he was above ground—no longer in the mine.

"No, that can't be," Mrs. Barnes gasped. "Howard has seniority."

I felt a lump grow in my throat.

The laid-off men hunched over and shuffled toward the crowd. Some had white tracks where tears ran down their blackened faces. They didn't even try to hide their emotions.

Mr. Ledford rubbed the tears from his face, turning the grimy soot into a ghostly mask. His wife was sick with lung cancer, what my grandma had died from. My mouth suddenly tasted like ash. Mrs. Ledford hadn't looked too good when I'd dropped off Mom's apple cobbler a few days earlier.

The crowd thinned as families walked home in silence.

My dad and his crew were the last ones out, as usual. As a supervisor, it was my dad's job to shut equipment down at the end of the day.

I felt a hand grip my shoulder. Mom stood next to me, clutching her coat tightly around her despite the warm sun. Her face was covered with shadows as she looked straight ahead. Mr. Ducat handed Dad his envelope.

Dad removed his ID tag from the board, rubbing his thumb over his initials and his number, 340, as if for good luck. Then he stared at the sealed envelope for what seemed like forever.

"Open it," I whispered.

Finally, he took a deep breath and ripped it open. He pulled out a paycheck, and nothing more. My dad still had his job, for now.

I sighed with relief. So did Mom. But my stomach hit my feet when Dad turned to face the men on his crew. I hadn't been watchin' them because I'd been staring at Dad so intently. But Uncle Bubba, Uncle Mike, Uncle

Rich, D.W., and Uncle Silas—that's what I called them, even though Uncle Bubba, Buster's dad, was the only one I was actually related to—every one of them held a pink slip. They stood together for the longest time, their eyes wide with shock. Nobody said a word as they patted each other's backs.

My eyes stung, but I couldn't even blink.

Mom hugged Aunt Livvy before she and Uncle Bubba left. Buster didn't even look up.

"Talk to ya later," I mumbled to Piran as Dad put an arm over me and Mom.

I was surprised to feel Dad actually leaning on me as we walked away. I glanced up. He coughed and blinked and looked away.

I didn't want to embarrass him, so I kept my eyes glued to my new sneakers. They were already scuffed and dirty.

CHAPTER 6
Crazy Ideas

Grandpa Chase was pacing on our front porch when we got home.

"I came straight over when I heard," he said and looked at Dad.

"I've still got my job," he said, "but I lost my crew, including Bubba."

"Damn." Grandpa patted him heavily on the back.

"Union is meetin' tomorrow," Dad said.

"I imagine so." Grandpa nodded.

"Pa, you going over to Livvy's?" Mom asked. "I was about to call her."

"Tell her I'll check on 'em tomorrow," he said. "I imagine they got enough to worry about tonight."

"Well, stay for dinner then," Mom muttered. "I'll get it going."

She made country-fried steak with mashed potatoes and gravy, which everybody usually loved. But we didn't eat much. I tried to enjoy it, but the meat stuck in my throat like a big lump that wouldn't go down.

Mom cleared the dishes and nodded toward Grandpa.

"Jack, let's you and me go set on the porch," he said.

I wanted to scream, *I'm thirteen for law's sake!* I hated when adults acted like I didn't know what was going on.

"String some beans while you're out there," Mom said and handed us two bowls, two peelers, and a bag of pole beans. Usually I'd complain, but this time I kept quiet.

Grandpa rocked the swing slowly back and forth—my sneakers brushing the porch floor with every pass. Between us, the bowls clicked softly against each other from our movement, sounding like a wind chime.

Grandpa snapped the ends off his beans and ran the peeler down each side twice as fast as I did. I tried to keep up, but I couldn't help listenin' to my parents arguing in the kitchen. They were upset and growing louder. I wondered how the other families were doing— the ones who'd gotten pink slips. We were lucky, but it didn't feel like it.

"Ow!" I said and stuck my knuckle in my mouth.

"Cut yourself?" Grandpa asked.

I nodded.

"Let's take a break," he said.

We sat back and watched the sun set over our Red Hills. The light turned the hilltops red, orange, and gold as the light hit them sideways and cast the erosion ditches into deep blues and purples. I suppose it was pretty in its own way—a lot of folks thought so.

Coppertown sat in a bowl at the southern tip of the Appalachian Mountains—they called it the Copper Basin. Low hills surrounded the town, and the Tohachee River cut from east to west through the middle of it like a zipper.

Since my dad was a supervisor, our house on Smelter Hill was high up. Not as high as the Rusts', but we had one of the better views around. I looked at the bridge that crossed to downtown with my school to the east, Tater Hill to the north, and the Company to the west—and at least fifty square miles of bare ground beyond that.

Folks were so proud when they'd talked about Coppertown on the national news. "The astronauts report they can see the denuded landscape of Coppertown, Tennessee, from the space shuttle." Course, that was before the *Challenger* blew up and they stopped flying 'em altogether.

We were known worldwide, but not for any reason I was proud of. It didn't seem right.

"Grandpa, since they closed up the smelting heaps, why haven't trees grown back?"

He cleared his throat and lowered his voice. "Well, Jack, the government put limits on the acid fumes allowed to escape the Company, but the folks who own it live far away in New York City, and they've never paid the rules much mind. As long as they're makin' their money..."

Those city people were treating us like the characters from *Star Trek* that nobody missed when they got zapped by lasers or eaten by aliens—the ones who hadn't been on the show long enough for anybody to care about 'em. They were expendable.

"It's not right!" I said.

"I know, Jack," Grandpa sighed. "But life is like that sometimes."

"Well, I want the trees back," I said. "I want a forest! So the roots can hold the ground together. Then maybe Uncle Amon wouldn't have died."

"Jack, the men work down in the rock, far below the dirt level," Grandpa said. "There's no tree on Earth whose roots could reach down that far."

"I… I don't care." I stretched to kick my foot on the porch, but caught mostly air.

It didn't make sense. We'd taken so much from Mother Nature. It seemed like she was just gettin' us back. Who would be next? Dad…or me?

"Someday, I'm gonna make the Company follow the rules," I said. "I'm gonna bring nature back."

Dad opened the screen door. "Pa, you fillin' his head with your crazy ideas again?"

"Ideas, my foot," Grandpa said. "You seen a bird around here lately?"

"The government tests the air all the time," Dad argued. "They say it's perfectly safe."

"What do you expect *them* to say with the Company wining and dining them every time they're here?" Grandpa said.

"It just ain't so, Pa. The Company takes good care of…" His voice trailed off.

"Yeah, like they took good care of your crew." Grandpa shook his head. "And like they took good care of Amon and your daddy. How many more need to die before you snap out o' yer fantasy, Ray?"

I froze.

Dad glared at Grandpa for a minute like he was going

to bust, but then his shoulders sank and he went back inside.

Dad was so proud of his job at the Company— the tradition, the money, the benefits—but sometimes I wondered if he was just coverin' up because he didn't know what else to do. Would he have been a miner if he'd had a choice? Would I have a choice?

CHAPTER 7

Sonny Rust

Everybody grew silent and stepped aside when Sonny Rust walked into school the next day. He looked like a deflating balloon shrinking into itself as he walked down the hall holding his books tight against him.

He turned toward his classroom but Buster blocked his path. "Where do you think you're goin'?"

Sonny refused to meet Buster's eyes and tried to meekly step around him, but Buster knocked his books out of his hands.

"You don't belong here anymore," Buster said through gritted teeth.

"I wouldn't have done it," Sonny squeaked and stared at the floor like he wished he could sink into it. "It wasn't me."

Buster's face turned red and his jaw muscles tensed like rubber bands—not good. I rushed to step between them. "Leave him alone, Buster." I may not have liked Sonny a whole lot, but I knew what my cousin was capable of when his temper let loose.

"Out of my way, cuz," Buster hissed.

"It wasn't his fault, Buster," I said. "He can't help that his dad is the Company manager. Just leave him alone, okay?" I could usually talk Buster down. I was one of the few people who could.

"Maybe you're right," Buster mumbled and looked down.

I sighed with relief.

"But I don't care!" Buster shouted. He stepped to the side then quickly spun around and nailed Sonny right in the eye with his fist. Sonny crumpled to the floor like a boneless chicken and slid into the wall.

"Send that message to your dad, you big turd," Buster growled.

Everybody started yelling at once, either "Stop, stop!" or "Hit him again! He deserves it!"

Miss Post's high-pitched voice cut through the chaos. "What is going on?"

Principal Slaughter was quickly in the middle of the

mess and grabbed Buster by the collar. "You're coming with me."

I offered Sonny my hand. "You okay?" He glanced at me with one hand covering his eye. It was already turning purple and swelling underneath.

"Yeah, thanks." He reached out as his chin quivered like he was about to cry.

"Don't listen to Buster," I said. "He's just sore because of his dad. He knows the layoffs weren't your fault."

"Maybe. But like he said, he doesn't care," Sonny muttered.

Miss Post put her arm around him. "Let's get you to the nurse," she said and smiled a *thank-you* back at me.

I watched them walk away. Sonny wasn't a completely bad guy. He was always around when you needed him to play shortstop or fill in on a math team. We just didn't *want* to *need* him. Like it or not, for us he stood for the Company. He reminded us how much we counted on the mine and how little choice we had about it.

Some people thought I did the right thing, helping Sonny out like that. They patted my back and grinned at me with nods. But some didn't. They bumped me hard when they walked by me in the hall or frowned before looking away.

"What were you thinking this mornin', huh, cuz? What about supporting your family?" Buster asked me that night when he called to chew me out. He'd been sent home early, so I hadn't seen him the rest of the school day.

"You would've killed him," I said.

"So?"

"Sonny's a pain in the butt, but he can't help who his parents are. And you don't need anything else on your record anyhow."

"So you were watchin' out for me, then?"

"In a way," I said. "I suppose."

There was a long silence. Finally, Buster said, "Well, all right then. We good?"

"Yeah, Buster, we're good."

I heard Aunt Livvy hollering at him in the background.

"I gotta go," Buster said. "I'm supposed to be grounded."

Mr. Rust pulled Sonny out of school the next day. Word was, they shipped him off to some private school in Chattanooga. I never saw him again.

Buster got three days' suspension, which wasn't much considerin'. I think the principal was quietly on his side. A lot of people wanted to beat the crap out of the Rusts. Buster just got there first.

CHAPTER 8
Slag Dump

My class shrank over the next two weeks from everybody's fathers who got laid off having to move their families somewhere else to find jobs. It seemed like every time I went to school somebody else was gone: Mathew Rymer, who played third base; Junior Meeks, who was sort of annoying but who I missed anyway; Lee Anne Rush, who was almost as pretty as Hannah—almost.

Miss Post tried to act like everything was normal, ignoring the empty chairs left in class, but nobody could pay attention.

I wondered about the places my friends were moving to. What would their new worlds look like? How green would they be? Would they have trees there? A guilty part of me felt a little bit jealous.

Then, one Friday on our way out of school, we saw that familiar glow coming from the Company.

"Slag dump!" Piran hollered.

Buster, Piran, and I took off runnin' for Tater Hill, stopping once for Piran to catch his breath. Our favorite rock ledge offered the best view of the train parked precariously close to the cliff edge as it tipped giant iron crucibles and let the hot molten rock flow down the cliff's side. The glowing lava spit sparks into the air and lit up the sky—our own private fireworks show—the color of Hannah's hair with the sunlight behind it. I couldn't stop gaping.

They'd been dumpin' slag for so many years that the Company actually sat on a small mountain of the cement-like stuff. Even so, I never got over watching a slag dump.

"Probably the last time I'll ever see this," Buster said.

Uncle Bubba had gotten a job at a chicken farm in Lumpkin.

"When yu'uns leaving?" Piran asked.

"Sunday after church," Buster said.

"Stan's moving too," Piran said. "His dad got a job in Cleveland."

"I heard Greg's family moved in with his aunt up in Murphy," I said.

"Damn, he was our best hitter," Piran replied. "We're running out of players."

"At least you'll be here to play," Buster grumbled.

At least you'll have trees, I almost said but bit my tongue. I was *supposed* to be feeling lucky for our lives not being upended like the lives of our friends who were havin' to move away.

We watched the lava turn black as it cooled.

"What about your house?" Piran asked. "You selling it?"

"Company house, we were just rentin' it. So all we gotta do is pack up and leave."

Miners switched houses like dominoes. Every time somebody got promoted, they'd move uphill, setting off a chain reaction as everybody below moved up a house too. The only reason we hadn't moved in a while was because Smelter Hill was as high as you could get. Except for the manager's house across town on Tater Hill where the Rusts lived—and no miner would ever live there.

So I was used to folks moving, just not *away* from Coppertown. They were like rats fleeing a sinking ship— except they weren't rats, they were my friends, and I didn't want to think of my home as a sinking anything.

CHAPTER 9

Tailings Pond

Next morning, Mom checked the weather in the backyard. She licked her finger and stuck it in the air to see how fast it dried. "Hmm… I think I can do laundry today."

"Where's Dad?" I asked.

"Down at Livvy and Bubba's helping load the truck," she said. "I'm heading over in a bit with some sandwiches and iced tea."

"I'm going to Piran's," I said.

"You ought to see if Buster wants to join you today, being his last day and all. I'm sure Livvy would appreciate him being out from underfoot. But yu'uns stay out of trouble, okay?"

"Yes, ma'am." *Tell that to Buster*, I thought. Buster was okay when he was calm, but I was tired of being his keeper when he wasn't, which was most of the time. It's why I wasn't too upset he was moving, though I'd miss Aunt Livvy and Uncle Bubba. Like Grandpa sometimes said, "You can pick yer friends, but you can't pick yer family."

It was a nice walk down Killer Hill—a little windy, but the sun was out so it wasn't too cold. The sky was a sharp blue against the orange hills and the river flashed shades of amber and brown as it rolled by me.

Wisps of fog were still burning off when I got down to the Quinns' house. It was always cooler at their place, being so close to the river. I got goose bumps as I walked to their front door, which was still in shadow. But it was warm inside.

"C'mon in, Jack," Mrs. Quinn hollered. I squeezed into their small kitchen as she yelled down the hall, "Piran, Jack's here." She returned to feeding something mushy and green to Piran's new little sister, Emily. Mom called her their "happy little accident."

Mr. Quinn pressed past me. "Morning, Jack. How are your parents holding up?"

"Morning, Mr. Quinn. Fine, I suppose."

Truth was, my parents didn't say much about the layoffs, not in front of me anyhow. Not that they had the time. Mom had been down at Aunt Livvy's helping her pack, and Dad was working a lot of overtime since the rest of his crew was gone.

"Should be a quiet day at the post office, honey. I won't be late." He kissed Mrs. Quinn on the cheek and Emily on the head before he left.

Emily started squalling just as Piran entered the kitchen, and the twins ran by in a blur, playing superheroes and chasing each other from room to room.

"Hey, Jack."

"God!" Hannah yelled from down the hall. "Can't anybody get some sleep around here?"

I looked to see if she was comin' out, but no such luck. The twins ran by again, shouting, "I killed you!" and "No you didn't!"

"Shut up already!" Hannah screamed.

"Watch your tongue, young lady," Mrs. Quinn hollered back.

"Emily cried all night." Piran rolled his eyes. "Let's get outta here before I get stuck babysitting. See ya later, Ma."

"Don't forget your inhaler!" she called behind us.

"What you want to do?" Piran asked as we walked back toward the bridge.

"I promised my mom we'd go get Buster," I said. Piran scrunched up his face.

"He can't possibly start a fight on his last day in town," I said.

"He better not."

We headed up Killer Hill and cut south on Poplar Trail.

"Have you ever noticed how roads are always named after whatever they cut down or chased off to put the road in?" I asked. "I mean, do you see any poplar trees? And our house is on Bear Ridge. What a joke."

"Yeah, but our house is on Lick Skillet Road, from when folks got so hungry during the Depression that they'd lick a hot skillet clean," Piran said. "That don't seem so funny to me."

I nodded and looked away. I got a lot of stomachaches, but never from hunger.

A long orange rental truck sat in front of Buster's house. Dad and Uncle Bubba were carrying a large trunk up the ramp.

"Livvy, what you got in this thing?" Uncle Bubba grunted.

"It's full of family heirlooms and they're breakable. Be careful," she said.

"Watch it there, Bubba," Dad called out from the depths of the truck bed. "You're about to crush me. Agh!"

"Oops, sorry, Ray."

Buster stood at the bottom of the ramp waiting with a box in his arms. His bottom lip stuck out like a little kid's.

"Aunt Livvy, you think you could do without Buster for a while?" I asked.

Buster looked at her with eyes big as dinner plates.

"Oh, go on," she said. "You've done plenty for today."

He smiled and dropped the box he was holding.

"Careful with that!" Aunt Livvy shouted. Her normally calm smile hid behind a deep frown.

Piran and I had to run to catch up with him at the end of the road.

"I didn't want to give her a chance to change her mind," he said. "Where we goin'?"

"Where do *you* want to go?" I asked. "Bein' yer last day and all."

"The tailings pond, the dry one, Old Number Two," Buster said.

Of course he would want to go where we weren't allowed on his last day here.

Piran and I looked at each other and shrugged. How could we say no?

We followed the railroad tracks out of town. My arm itched like wildfire as we passed the trestle bridge, though luckily Eli and his friends weren't around.

"Dare you to cross!" Buster laughed loudly at his own lame joke.

"Not funny," I groaned. Piran shook his head.

The only thing that was supposed to keep people out of the Old Number 2 Tailings Pond was a faded DANGER sign on the gate that blocked the dirt road leading in. We followed the well-worn path that hooked around it to the right and walked to the edge of the pond. I stared at the expanse of wasteland with its out-of-this-world look. So much of our world was out of whack lately that it seemed a fittin' place to be.

Buster hoisted an imaginary machine gun and danced across the pond. "*Pow, pow, pow, pow, pow.* Enemy fire incomin'!"

Piran and I blasted back with our laser guns.

"Silly human, you don't stand a chance against our advanced weaponry. *Pew, pew, pew!*"

Suddenly, an engine roared and a shiny new yellow Jeep with enormous bumpy tires lunged into view.

"Duck!" Piran yelled.

We dove behind a large rock to hide and watched the

Jeep do doughnuts around the tailings pond, kicking up clouds of the fine silicone dirt. Given the direction the wind was blowin', the dirt would be coating our parents' cars back home before it settled down.

It might even coat the moving van as a going-away present.

The Jeep's back tires sank deep into the ground once, but it pulled out before it sank farther. The ground wasn't stable—which is why the DANGER sign was there, and why we *weren't* supposed to be there, as far as our parents were concerned. And yet, here were a bunch of whoopin' idiots riding around in a big, heavy vehicle.

"I don't believe our bad luck!" Piran shouted over the noise. "Eli Munroe! How's he got the money to buy that brand-new Jeep?"

"Don't know. Dad said the mine wouldn't hire him... before the layoffs," I said. "And I saw him get fired from the gas station." I hadn't heard of him working anywhere else either.

"Why are we hiding?" Buster said. "You ain't scared of him because of what happened at the trestle bridge, is ya? We were here first. We could try to run 'em off."

"I swear, Buster, keepin' you out of trouble is a full-time job," I said. "Just keep down, y'hear?"

Buster's face clouded over. "Don't worry. I won't be your *job* for much longer."

"That's not what I meant…" I started to say, but his attention was already back on Eli.

I couldn't help but compare the two. Was Eli like Buster, all brash and no common sense? Or was he just a guy whose dream had been ripped away? Eli wanted to be a miner—he'd even quit school to become a miner—but they wouldn't hire him. Now he seemed to have nothing to do—or at least nothing good.

Without the mine, was I going to turn out like Eli? Was that my future too?

As soon as church let out the next day, we headed over to Aunt Livvy and Uncle Bubba's house again. The truck was full to the top but Uncle Bubba managed to squeeze in one last box anyway. The chairs and tables that used to decorate their home looked sad wedged together like a bunch of unimportant clutter—the oak dining table where they'd spent a lifetime of meals, the chair with the chipped corner from when Buster broke his tooth on it as a kid, the plaid couch where they took their Christmas photo last year.

Could our entire life fit into one truck like that?

Buster leaned against his family's station wagon, slamming a ball into his glove again and again.

"Hey," I said as I leaned against the car next to him.

"Hey," he mumbled, his lip sticking out again.

Uncle Bubba pulled down the cargo door of the truck and brushed off his hands. "I guess that's it, then."

Aunt Livvy and Mom hugged and burst into tears.

"Women," Buster and I said at the same time.

I looked at him sideways. "Good luck, Buster. Really. And try to stay out of trouble, will ya?" I smiled.

"Yeah, okay." An expression passed over his face that I'd never seen before—something different from his usual rock-hard scowl. His chin started shaking and... Was he trying not to cry? I shifted my feet and looked the other way.

"Let me know what happens with the Union," Uncle Bubba said to Dad.

"Will do," Dad said.

They shook hands goodbye, so Buster and I did too. But our mothers insisted on hugging everybody and soaked our shirts with their tears. "We'll see yu'uns at Thanksgiving," they both sobbed.

Uncle Bubba climbed into the truck and Aunt Livvy

and Buster loaded into their station wagon. Mom, Dad, and I waved as they drove off down Poplar Trail. Mom kept wipin' her eyes.

"Grace, they're only going to be an hour-and-a-half drive away," Dad said. "It's not like you won't ever see your sister again."

"I know," she said. "But it won't be the same."

I agreed. And somehow, I was feeling left behind.

CHAPTER 10
Halloween

A cold snap snuck in as Halloween drew closer. The sky turned a brilliant blue, making the orange landscape stand out even more. Along with the sulfur, the smell of fireplace smoke drifted through the air.

Mom and Dad weren't saying much to each other, and the air in our house felt thick as mud with all the silence. Not that they had much chance to talk if they'd wanted to. Between Dad workin' so much overtime and all the Union meetings, I barely saw him anymore. So I was surprised when early one Saturday he woke me up and said, "Let's go get us a pumpkin, Jack."

That meant going to the Spencer farm outside of Coppertown!

We drove west through the Tohachee River Gorge along the winding road that was cut into the cliff and ran dangerously close to the water's edge. Semitrucks passed us from time to time, nearly pushin' us against the rock wall. Dad said it was the only road running east to west through the mountains, so the trucks had to use it—there was no other way through.

When trucks weren't blocking our view, I watched the river. It broke into foamy rapids over enormous boulders as it rushed through the gorge. The slope on the far side was covered in tall trees whose leaves had turned all different colors. It looked like a giant bowl of Fruity Pebbles cereal—even the rapids looked like milk runnin' through the middle.

I kept turning my head this way and that—I didn't want to miss a thing.

Classic country music spilled out of the radio—June and Anita Carter, Johnny Cash, Patsy Cline. Mom sang along to all of it. Dad reached for her hand and I leaned back in my seat, enjoying the break from the tension that had been growing in our house.

When we got to the Spencer farm, yellow, red, and purple leaves skittered across the parking lot like small animals. I chased after them, collecting a handful of perfect specimens, and showed 'em to Mom. She'd spent her summers as a little girl with her grandparents up on

Beech Mountain in North Carolina, so she knew a thing or two about plants—even if her garden never did very well.

"This is a sugar maple," she said. "You can tell by how yellow it is and its points. And that's an oak leaf." It had more rounded edges and was deeply cut in. "And this is a tulip poplar." It was what Buster's road was named after. It looked alien and fat compared to the others.

Even though Miss Post's quiz on trees was long past, I was still interested. And the real things looked way better than any pictures in a book.

"I want to keep 'em," I said.

"They'll dry out and turn brown if you leave them exposed," Mom said.

She reached into the back seat and handed me her Bible, which she hadn't removed from the car since church last Sunday. "Here, press them between the pages. That'll help preserve 'em longer."

I carefully held the stems as I placed the maple leaf nice and flat in Genesis, the oak leaf in Psalms, and the tulip poplar in Revelations. Now if I could just tell which trees they'd come from—the edge of the parking lot was thick with them. Most were a mystery, but the sugar maple stood out like a bright flame against the others. I stopped breathing it was so beautiful.

"C'mon, Jack—pumpkins!" Dad said, snapping me out of my thoughts. Next to the big Spencer barn, pumpkins of all shades of orange were lined up in three groups—small, medium, and large.

Mom put her hand on my back and steered me toward the smaller pumpkins. "Aren't they cute?"

"Grace, as long as I've got a job, he can have any damned pumpkin he wants," Dad said. Quick as that, the tension was back, turning my stomach to knots.

I chose a pumpkin from the middle section—a medium-sized one. From a distance, it looked almost perfectly round, with a curly stem on top. Up close, one side of it was kind of flat, but if I turned that part to the back, no one would notice. It would do.

Dad said, "I saw you eyin' that big one over there, Jack. Let's get that one."

I glanced at Mom.

"You picked out a fine pumpkin, Jack," she said and glared at Dad. "And I bet it will still be the biggest pumpkin in Coppertown *this* Halloween."

I tried to ignore the look that passed between them, but Dad's red face was hard to unsee. He carried the medium pumpkin to the car, which took longer than it should have. When he came back, he was back to his normal color but his eyes were shiny. His moods flipped like pancakes these days.

How many fewer pumpkins will there be in Coppertown this Halloween? I wondered. *Since so many folks probably can't afford 'em.*

Mom got some fresh squash and greens from the produce stand. Dad bought a Styrofoam cup full of boiled peanuts. We sat on the car hood slurping and munching the hot nuts. Salty juice dripped down my sleeves as I sucked the meat from the shells and tossed them to the ground. The salt made my fingers tingle as they went from the warm peanuts to the cold, crisp air over and over again. We went through the entire cup in no time, but I didn't ask for more.

The ride home was quieter than the ride over. Mom and Dad didn't hold hands and she didn't sing along with the radio. They looked straight ahead while I watched the trees thin out as we got closer to home, back to our Red Hills.

Out of the gorge and about thirty minutes west of Coppertown we saw Eli Munroe in his shiny new Jeep cutting up a side road.

"I wonder where he's going to?" Dad said.

"Maybe he's getting a pumpkin too," I replied, though that didn't seem like something Eli would ever care about.

I watched Dad's brow furrow in the rearview mirror. "Ain't no pumpkins that way."

After dinner, Dad and I cut off the top of the pumpkin and cleaned out the guts with big spoons. We squished the goo between our fingers to pull out the seeds, which Mom roasted in the oven. I carved a scary face into the pumpkin's good side and laughed as Dad tried to imitate its lopsided expression. The good mood from earlier that day seeped back in as Mom put a small candle inside and set the pumpkin on the front stoop.

"That's a fine jack-o'-lantern," Dad said and put his hand on my shoulder.

"You did a good job on the design, honey." Mom nodded at Dad as if to say, *See?*

I smiled and crunched on the hot pumpkin seeds until my gums went raw from the salt.

Piran and I were too old to wear goofy costumes for Halloween anymore—we had to be cool. So we dressed like fighter pilots from the movie *Top Gun*. I borrowed Grandpa's World War II leather bomber jacket. Piran wore coveralls. We put on sunglasses and strutted around like bulls.

Everybody did their trick-or-treating downtown, since the county was so spread out. Business owners set up tables in front of their stores and gave out candy by the bucketload. Kids came from all over. Sheriff Elder led the parade down Water Street in his police cruiser with his lights flashin' and him shouting "Happy Halloween" over his intercom. The fire department was right behind him in their big red fire truck. Piran and I walked with the crowd of goblins, witches, and superheroes following behind that. There were so many folks in the parade, there weren't many left to line the streets.

Piran and I entered the costume contest, but the prize for our age group went to Bill Worley, who dressed as the best zombie I'd ever seen. I entered my pumpkin in the carving contest and won second prize. Turned out, there were a few pumpkins in Coppertown after all. And we both bobbed for apples—I took off Grandpa's jacket for that. And of course there was the candy.

But even with a county's worth of kids, it seemed smaller than the year before. Mostly folks were handing out suckers, Bit-O-Honeys, and Tootsie Rolls—the cheap stuff. And the Company table, which always had the best candy, wasn't there at all.

So when somebody hollered, "Hey, Dilbeck's Pharmacy is giving out chocolate bars!" Piran and I both made a beeline straight for their table, even though I was the chocolate nut. We went back three times before Mrs. Dilbeck told us to shoo.

We made our way back to where the Quinns were set up in front of the post office. They only gave out SweeTarts, but they still had a crowd. Hannah dressed up as a witch with striped stockings and a drooping black hat that made her look like a movie star. Even with Emily sitting on her hip, wicked had never looked so good.

"Piran, have you seen the twins?" Mrs. Quinn asked.

We turned just in time to spot Superman chasing Batman through the crowd with a light saber.

"Oh, there they are," Mrs. Quinn said. "Okay."

"Hi, Hannah. How's it goin'?" I asked and tripped over the foot of the card table. Piran guffawed and nearly spit out his candy. I shot him an evil look as I quickly made my escape into the crowd before she could answer.

Piran caught up with me and slapped me on the

back—still laughing. But his smile died when we found ourselves trailing close behind Eli and overheard his friends talking about Hannah. It wasn't anything that should ever be said about a pretty girl or any girl for that matter, and certainly not about Piran's sister.

I looked at Piran. His lips were pressed tightly together and his fists were clenched. He was about to step forward and say something when Eli cut them off and said, "Don't talk about her like that. Besides, I got good news about our latest crop."

I grabbed Piran's arm and whispered, "Crop of what?" Eli was no farmer.

Will McCaffrey turned around and looked at us with murder in his eyes. Then he recognized me. "Jack, yu'uns back off. This hain't nothin' to do with you." He put his hand on my chest and gave me a small push. "For your own good."

Piran and I froze with our mouths hanging open. *Did he just threaten us?*

"What was that about?" Piran asked, but then he got distracted by a bucket full of bubble gum in front of Faysal's Dress Shop. After several more laps through town, we sat on the bridge to sort through our loot.

"I'll trade you three suckers for that Snickers," I said.

"Okay," Piran replied around a mouth full of Bit-O-Honey. "Trade you a Baby Ruth for that there taffy." He never did have expensive taste in candy.

At the end of the bridge I spied Eli Munroe pulling Hannah into the shadows. Giggling, they looked around suspiciously.

No.

"There's…there's Hannah." I pointed. "With Eli." My mouth went dry.

"Oh man. Dad is not going to be happy if she starts going out with *him*."

"How could she?" I stared. "He doesn't have enough sense to spit downwind."

"You're a much better catch." Piran nodded. "Even if you are a goober. Speakin' of which…"

He grabbed the small packet of chocolate-covered peanuts from my stash. I didn't mind. I suddenly didn't want any of it.

Of course, I might have been full.

I held my belly and moaned as I wobbled home with my parents, my loot, and my pumpkin with its second-place ribbon.

"I told you not to eat so much candy," Mom said. "You *can* save some for later, you know."

My eyes rolled in my head.

Dad leaned over and peeked in my bag. "You got an extra candy bar in there for me?"

"Ray!" Mom swatted at him.

When I crawled into bed, my stomach still ached like I'd been poisoned. So did my heart. Eli and Hannah. Surely, it couldn't last.

CHAPTER 11
Strike

A few nights later, Dad arrived home late—again. "There are only three hundred of us left," he complained over his fried chicken, "and they expect us to keep up the same pace as before the layoffs. Do you believe it? They've got us doin' jobs we weren't trained to do. They had me driving a backhoe today. It's been so long, I barely remember how. It's dangerous, I tell ya." He shook his head. "I need my crew."

Mom's forehead wrinkled with worry. Two men had already left the mines in ambulances since the workforce had been cut. Dad didn't talk about it. It was like losing Amon all over again—and again, and again.

The phone rang, the harsh sound making us jump.

"Hello?" A wide grin spread across Dad's face. "Heck yeah, we'll be there." He turned to us. "It's about damn time. The Union's made a decision. They're calling a meeting at the community center tomorrow at seven."

"Jack, would you be okay home alone?" Mom asked.

"Grace, this affects him too," Dad replied. "Besides, if he's going to be a miner someday, he needs to start making friends with the Union."

He got back on the phone and called more miners to help get the word out. I looked down at my hands, which were suddenly numb.

I didn't sleep that night. It rained, which made my arm ache, and I couldn't stop thinking about what Dad said. I imagined about a dozen different ways of telling him I didn't want to be a miner, but they all turned out bad.

The next night, I stood with my parents, buried in the crowd of thick, rugged miners. With their blue jeans and plaid flannel shirts, they reminded me of the gnarled old oak trees from Miss Post's slideshow—mad oak trees, with their muscles tensed up and fire in their eyes.

Despite the cold outside, it was hot and humid inside. Steam rose off the miners as they shook their fists and shouted, "They can't do this to us!"

"I need my crew back," Dad yelled. "I can't do that job by myself! It's not safe!"

"They own the whole town. How can we fight?" Mr. Barnes asked.

Mr. Hill shouted, "We STRIKE!"

A roar of agreement rolled around the room like thunder. There was no discussion. It was what everybody had been waitin' for. And I was getting my wish. If the miners were on strike, Dad wouldn't have to be underground no more.

The Union organized everything. They signed up the men who weren't on unemployment for stipends, or strike pay, and scheduled times for people to walk the picket lines. I helped make signs for the men to carry.

"Gotta make it right for the next round of miners," I heard someone say as they slapped my back. I coughed and Mom looked at me with that same worried expression.

Could I tell her how I felt?

The miners were fired up. It was scary, but exciting too. The men were loyal and close, like my baseball team. Their energy ran through me like a train. Soon I was yellin' right along with them. Our voices echoed off the walls like drums: "STRIKE, STRIKE, STRIKE!"

We went straight to the Company store after the meeting.

Dad said, "We need to stock up in case things get tough."

"Tough how?" I asked.

"The Company isn't gonna be real happy about this strike," he said. "Back when your grandpa Chase was working the mine, the workers went on strike to force the Union in, and the Company shut down the store to make things hard on 'em. But folks were one step ahead and stocked up before the strike. So that's what we're going to do—stock up. We gotta get there before the Company catches wind of the plan."

I loved the Company store. They had the best of everything, even the BMX dirt bike I wanted, which sat in the corner, shiny green with knobby tires. I tried not to stare.

Everybody shopped at the Company store, but miners' families got a discount. Every now and then Mom would drive to the city to find something specific, but not often. That's why it was so easy to pick out the mining families in town—they were almost always the best dressed and had the latest everything. Of course, we already knew who they were anyway.

We weren't alone when we got to the store. I helped my parents quickly fill a basket to overflowing with things like tuna fish, coffee, toilet paper, flour, yeast, and soap—things that would last a long time. We managed to get in the checkout line not too far back. It quickly grew behind us and wrapped around the shelves, which were now almost bare.

Mr. Ledford stood at the checkout counter with a small selection of goods.

"He's lost weight since I dropped by last week," Mom whispered. "Poor man is trying to take care of his wife without any nursing help."

We were close enough that I overheard Mr. Ledford ask, "What do you mean I can't buy groceries?"

"You can't buy on credit anymore," Mr. Davenport said loudly. "You've got nothin' for it to come out of."

"I don't have any cash," Mr. Ledford muttered. "My last paycheck was only ten dollars."

"You and half the other men," Mr. Davenport replied. "We were doin' you a favor lettin' you charge against it all this time."

"My wife got sick," Mr. Ledford said. "I got behind."

"That's not my problem," Mr. Davenport said. "Now step aside, so I can ring up the Hills."

Mr. Ledford just stood there with his mouth open.

"Saint Peter don't call me 'cause I can't go. I owe my soul to the Company store," Dad said, quoting the Tennessee Ernie Ford tune.

"Mom, can we help?" I asked.

She already had her wallet open. Dad nodded as she pulled out a few dollars. I pulled two wadded up bills out of my pocket to add to it. Up and down the line of grocery carts, families pulled money from their wallets and passed it forward. By the time it got to the front it was a thick bundle of cash—enough for several trips to the store.

Mr. Hill slapped the pile on the counter and said, "Mr. Ledford has plenty of money to buy his groceries. I suggest you check him out now."

Mr. Ledford gave everyone the slightest nod. His eyes were wide and brimming with tears as he turned back around like a turtle pulling into his shell. He paid for his groceries and quickly left the store.

I was never so proud of my neighbors. But Mr. Ledford was a scary reminder of how close any of us were to being in a similar situation.

Dad still left for the mine every morning, but now it was to strike at the front gate…*where he can't get hurt*, I thought, but rubbed my lucky rabbit's foot anyway.

Piran and I stood on the bridge after school and watched the miners picketing in the distance. The men chanted and punched the sky with their signs as they circled in front of the Company.

Dad came home excited at the end of the day. "We'll have our jobs back in no time—all of us. They'll give in soon."

Was it wrong of me to hope not?

By Thanksgiving, Dad was a little less fired up. "They're not makin' any money without the Company running. They need us back," he said. "They've got to compromise."

I almost envied Buster when his family came over for Thanksgiving. Living on a chicken farm might not have been so great, but at least they knew what tomorrow looked like. His dad had a job, and they could always eat chicken.

CHAPTER 12

December

Now Jack, I don't want you getting your hopes up about Christmas, y'hear?" Mom said on the way to the Piggly Wiggly one Saturday. The Company had shut down the store like Dad predicted, so we had to drive forty minutes out of town for groceries, even though we didn't buy that much. "We don't have the money to spend this year like we used to."

The Christmas season had moved in with a lot less celebration than normal. The town put up twinkle lights, but with the miners still on strike, everybody was hurtin'. The storefronts didn't have anything new in the windows and holiday spirits were low.

"I know," I replied, although I ached for that BMX dirt bike that would have been mine if things were different. I tried my best not to be bitter about it, but our minister, Father Huckabay, would have had a field day if he could peek inside my head. I knew I was luckier than most and tried to count my blessings. Really, I did.

We passed Crazy Coote on the way out of town. He looked right at me like he could read my mind. I shrank into my seat, feeling guilty for wantin' anything at all.

As we followed the Tohachee River northeast over the mountains, the scenery changed from our paper-bag landscape to something very different. Pastures full of woolly cows nibbling on weeds and brown grass came into view. Bare trees stretched their skeletal branches up to the pale gray sky. Even without their leaves, they were beautiful, like living sculptures.

"What do you suppose trees do all winter?" I asked Mom. "Do they sleep?"

"Not really. They concentrate all their growing underground when it's too cold above."

They looked to be hibernating. But not all the trees were bare. Small evergreens grew along the pasture fences. "What kind of trees are those green ones there?"

"Those are spruce trees," she said. "Birds eat the seeds, land on the fences, and well, they poop. It's fertilizer and a seed in one. So that's where the trees grow."

"Then they're bird-crap trees?" I said and quickly covered my mouth.

"Jack!" She glared at me but then turned away. I could see her grin in the window's reflection.

"We gonna have a Christmas tree this year at least?" I begged.

"No, Jack, that's wasted money," she said with the frown again. "I'm sorry, but I need you to be mature about this for me, okay? Just this year, please?"

Being poor sucked. Still, I couldn't stop thinkin' about bird-crap trees. If we could just get birds to fly over Coppertown, maybe they'd help make trees. I'd take bird-crap trees over no trees at all.

Dad showed up a week before Christmas with a tree tied to the roof of the family car anyway. Puffed up like a rooster, with an axe in his hand, he planted it on the ground next to him with a proud "Ta-da!"

He looked like Paul Bunyan in his denim and plaid flannel top. Mom snickered, "Oh, Ray, what have you done?"

It was a bird-crap tree. My dad brought home a bird-crap tree for Christmas. *Well, don't that just beat all.*

We set it up inside anyhow and tried to decorate it, but the branches were too floppy to hold any ornaments. So we threw tinsel over it and called it done.

As we stood staring at it, Mom covered her mouth and tried not to laugh. It was contagious. I squeezed my lips tight to keep from busting up.

Finally Dad said, "Well ain't that the saddest lookin' Christmas tree yu'uns ever seen?"

That was all it took. We laughed until tears ran down our faces.

I didn't realize how long it had been since I'd heard my parents make that sound.

I couldn't imagine not giving my family something for Christmas, but I didn't have any money since Mom cut my allowance. I looked around my bedroom hoping for an idea. And there it was in the bottom drawer of my desk.

I pulled out my old sketch pad and some colored pencils. I hadn't used them since I was a kid, but I didn't have anything else. So I drew a landscape of Coppertown for Dad. I used up half my yellow and orange trying to get the land to look just right. For Mom, I drew a bird. It had to be a sparrow, like in the tune she always sang. I looked it up in a book I'd checked out from the school library and was surprised at the picture. The bird was small, brown, and gray, nothing special to look at.

"Its charming song belies its dull appearance," the book said. Maybe the next time we left Coppertown I could try to hear one. Unless they migrated. Wasn't that what birds did?

I'll add some colors and make it prettier.

I did one more landscape drawing of Coppertown, this one for Grandpa, but this time I added trees using lots of greens and blues. That one was the most fun to do as I imagined my home the way it used to be before the mining started. I wanted Grandpa to see it that way too.

I smiled at my drawings—they looked all right. I signed each one "Love, Jack," rolled them up, and tied some kitchen string around them.

I was so proud of myself that I felt like a turkey with its tail fanned out. I went to find my parents, not to tell 'em what I'd done but just to hint a little maybe. Mom was in their bedroom with the door closed. I knocked. "Mom?"

"Don't come in!" she yelled and made sounds that made me think of juggling Tupperware.

I frowned. "Well, where's Dad?"

"I think he's out in his metal shop."

That was where he always was now, if he wasn't picketing. He'd come home from the strike, take a shower, and go out to his shop. If it weren't for dinner, I'd probably never see him. The message was clear—he wanted to be alone.

I sighed and went to the kitchen for a snack. There wasn't much in the fridge, or in the cabinets neither, just stuff that had to be cooked, like beans, soup, and rice. I finally found a jar of peanut butter. *That'll do.* I took a spoon, scooped out a big hunk, and ate it like a Popsicle.

Lately it seemed like I was hungry all the time, and there was never enough food around. Mom said I was gonna eat us out of house and home. It made me feel awful, but how was I supposed to stop growing?

CHAPTER 13
Christmas

W e went to church on Christmas Eve, as usual. The choir sang carols out of tune, as usual. The room did look nice with the twinkle lights and candles lit, though. There was a real Christmas tree in the back of the church. It filled the air with its spicy scent, which mingled with cinnamon and hot apple cider. Everybody was dressed in their Sunday best, which made it feel more festive.

Piran and I laughed about everyone huggin' and shaking hands like they didn't see each other every Sunday anyway. The smiles may have been more forced than usual, but everybody seemed to be trying. Anytime the word "strike" was mentioned, somebody got finger-smacked on the arm or back, or even on the back of their head if they didn't stop.

Then I spotted Hannah. All the twinkle lights framed her, lighting her up all golden and sparkly. Her friends sounded like a pack of hens out at the Spencer farm, but she just smiled and outshined them like copper in the ore, a diamond in the coal, the jewel that she was.

Could she feel me looking at her? I'd grown an inch recently—would she notice? I willed her to glance my way, but her eyes kept straying toward the back of the church. I followed her gaze to Eli Munroe. He stood near the door with his parents like a black cloud.

What does she see in that guy?

He was dressed in a suit—one that actually fit him, unlike mine, which was feeling a little tight. And he looked right back at Hannah with…with love in his eyes. Surely Eli couldn't feel anything that deeply—even though that's what it looked like.

She'll figure him out soon enough. She'll see him for what he really is, and I'll have my chance. I just hoped it would be soon.

Back home, we did our traditional reading of "The Night Before Christmas," with sound effects. I especially liked pounding on things during "the prancing and pawing of each little hoof." It was a very noisy poem, what with all the snorin' and whistling and such. Of course, I didn't tell any of my friends that we did that. I would have been laughed out of the county.

"What about milk and cookies for Santa?" I asked. Yeah, I'd been too old for Santa for a while, but we always pretended I wasn't. It was part of the Christmas fun.

"Not this year," Mom replied and squeezed my shoulder. I went to bed feeling lower than a sunken mine. *A bird-crap Christmas tree, no cookies, and no bike—this is going to be the worst Christmas ever.*

Christmas morning I grabbed my drawings and ran for the den. *Maybe, just maybe.*

I stopped short and sighed when I saw the tree. Santa had definitely skipped us. Two gifts wrapped in brown paper and tied up with kitchen string sat next to the tree. Nothing else, no dirt bike. Not that I really expected it, but I had hoped anyway.

"Maybe we can get your bike next year." Mom hugged me from behind.

"How'd you know?" I asked. I'd made a point of not saying anything about it recently, although I'd worn out the magazine in my bedside drawer staring at the ad.

"Merry Christmas!" Dad shouted as he entered the room. "Well, lookie there, presents! You better open 'em, Jack."

I tucked my drawings in with the gifts and shook off my bad mood as best I could. I tried to fetch the larger of the two packages, but it wouldn't budge. I had to leave it on the floor to rip off the paper. Underneath was a handmade model of the General Lee from *The Dukes of Hazzard*.

"It must weigh fifty pounds!" I grunted as I lifted it out.

"Close to it," Dad said.

"So that's what you've been up to in your metal shop." Mom smiled.

Dad had cut every piece, welded and riveted them together, painted the car a deep orange, and even hand-painted the rebel flag on its roof. It looked like a miniature version of the real thing. He'd done a beautiful job.

"Wow," I said, admiring his work.

"It's your favorite, right?" Dad asked.

"Oh yeah," I said, smiling. "Thanks, Dad!" I tried to

roll it across the floor, but the round wheels scratched the wood. Dad could do anything with metal, but he couldn't make tires. If he could've, it woulda saved a lot of money since cars in Coppertown went through tires fast.

"It's kind of more for display," Dad said.

"I'll find a good spot for it." I smiled. I knew I'd be staring at it a lot, dreaming of myself at the wheel.

"You have more," Mom said and handed me the other package, which was large and squishy.

I tore off the paper and pulled out a multicolored quilt. I ran my hand over the bumpy and uneven surface—it felt soft and somewhat worn. I stared at a blue patch with white writing.

"Hey, that's my old baseball team, the Braves!" Another patch looked like my first pajamas. "What the…?"

"I took your old clothes, the ones that I could never throw away, and made a quilt out of 'em," Mom said with a sniff.

I held it up and looked closely. "That was the back pocket on my favorite overalls, the ones with the patch, and that was my favorite shirt when I was a kid." It was a fabric scrapbook of my life. "Mom, this is really nice, thanks."

"Grace, I didn't know you quilted," Dad said.

"I didn't either." She blushed.

Dad handed her a small box. "Ray! I thought we agreed no presents!" She glared at him but untied the string and opened the lid anyway. Inside was a Christmas tree formed by silver waves going back and forth.

"Oh no, Ray, this is too expensive." She frowned. "You shouldn't have."

"Don't worry, Gracie. I made it myself out of stainless steel wire. I hammered the shape." Dad pulled it out of the box by the black ribbon he'd run through the loop at the top. "See here, it's a charm necklace." He tied it around her neck.

Mom smiled wide and tears ran down her cheeks. She threw her arms around my dad and gave him a huge kiss...which kept going.

I coughed...then coughed again a little more loudly.

"Sorry!" They smiled.

"I've got something for yu'uns too."

"Really?"

I handed them my rolled-up drawings.

"I didn't know we had an artist in the family," Dad said.

"Oh, Jack, it's wonderful," Mom said. "What kind of bird is it?"

"It's a sparrow, like in your song," I replied. "But I thought I'd make it prettier, so I colored it purple."

"It's beautiful, honey. Thank you." She hugged me tight, wrapping me in her smell of soap and flour. "We've got to hang them somewhere." She grabbed some pins from the bedroom and Dad tacked them on the wall above the couch.

"That looks real nice," he said. We stared at my picture of the barren landscape of Coppertown next to the sparrow—two things that didn't go together anywhere but on our wall.

"I'll start breakfast," Mom said and wiped the tears from her cheeks.

She made biscuits and gravy with eggs, grits, and sausage roll—the biggest breakfast we'd had in a long while. It wouldn't have been Christmas without sausage

roll—the pin-wheeled pastries smothered with ketchup were a family tradition. I added hot sauce to my ketchup like Dad did and it burned on my tongue.

Grandpa showed up halfway through breakfast with an armful of presents. He handed Mom a bag of oranges, which she set to slicing up. He handed me a fishing pole tied with a big red bow. "I couldn't for the life of me figure out how to wrap it," he said.

"Cool, Grandpa. Thanks!" Now Piran and I would both have one for the summer, although it would be a while before we'd be able to use 'em.

"Grace, sit for two seconds," he said. "I got you somethin' better than oranges." Mom dried her hands on the kitchen towel and unwrapped a camel-hair coat. "Oh, Pa, thank you."

"I got it at Faysal's Dress Shop," he said. "Your old one was lookin' a little bit moth-eaten, and sometimes you got to treat yourself to the nicer things rather than givin' it all away to everybody else." He looked at her with a knowing expression and Mom blushed.

He gave Dad a metric ratchet set for his metal shop—about the only thing he didn't already have.

"How'd you know?" The tops of Dad's ears turned red, a sure sign he was pleased.

I showed Grandpa my General Lee, and Mom showed him her Christmas-tree charm.

"You made these?" Grandpa's eyebrows went up. "Nice work, Ray. If you make some more of these, I'll try to sell 'em in my store." That was a high compliment.

"And look what Mom made for me," I said and showed him the quilt. I pointed out all the pieces and told him where they'd come from.

He touched it gingerly, like it was a treasure. "Grace, you think you could make one of these for me from your mama's old dresses?" Mom looked at him, surprised. Grandpa Chase didn't mention Grandma very often. Even now it was still painful for him. "I'd pay ya, of course," he said.

"You wouldn't have to pay me, Pa. I'd be happy to."

"Nonsense. I know yu'uns could use the money, and it would mean the world to me."

"All right." Mom wrung the kitchen towel between her hands tightly. She didn't talk about her mother much either, 'cept for her singin'. Mom claimed Grandma Chase had an even prettier voice than she did, which I found hard to believe. I'm sure I'd heard her sing, but most of my memories of Grandma Chase were like an out-of-focus slideshow.

While my parents cleaned up, I handed Grandpa my drawing. "It's Coppertown, Grandpa, the way it used to be. The way it'll be again someday." *Somehow.*

"This is right handsome, Jack," he said. I could have sworn I saw his eyes water up before he looked away. He hugged me so tight, I thought I was gonna break.

Grandpa asked to see some of Dad's other projects in his metal shop while Mom made a green-bean casserole, yeast rolls, and apple pie.

"That's not all we're having, is it?" I asked. Our meals had been pretty slim lately, so I was worried.

"No, Jack." Mom laughed. "Everybody's bringing a dish just like at Thanksgiving. It'll add up, you'll see. We're not going hungry quite yet."

Speak for yourself, I thought.

The whole family showed up at our place again, 'cept Aunt Catherine, who never did come back, and Uncle Amon, of course. I caught Dad lookin' out the window, all wistful, a few times.

Mom was right—we ended up with a feast. Since Uncle Bubba was a hunter, he brought a wild turkey. Aunt Livvy made giblet gravy, sweet potatoes with marshmallows, regular mashed potatoes, and pumpkin pie. She brought brussels sprouts too, but I didn't eat any of those.

Grandpa brought the cranberry sauce and I helped him get it out of the can in one ringed piece.

Dad and Bubba started talking about the strike over dinner, but Aunt Livvy told them to shush. "It's Christmas. Yu'uns give it a rest."

Buster and I sat at the card table, even though we were too big for it. Course, there weren't no room at the big table for all the adults and us too.

"How do you like your new place?" I asked him.

"It's okay, I suppose," he said, "'cept for when the wind blows the wrong way. Those chickens stink something awful. Worse than a sulfur cloud."

"There haven't been any of those since the miners went on strike," I whispered. "The whole plant is shut down."

His eyebrows went up at that. "That don't sound normal."

"It's not." I smiled.

After dinner, Grandpa played Christmas carols on his fiddle and we sang along.

That night, I crawled into bed full and tired and wrapped up in the quilt Mom made for me. I didn't get a lot of presents like other years, or my BMX bike, but everything I got came straight from the heart and it felt pretty good.

The week sped by visiting with friends, but New Year's Eve snuck through quiet as a mouse. I heard a few bottle rockets here and there, but mostly people let the New Year in with as little notice as possible. So much time had gone by since the strike began that people were startin' to worry, and without the holidays to think about, it crept back into everybody's heads. My parents didn't say much in front of me, but I could hear them whispering in their bedroom at night. Whatever they were saying, it didn't sound good.

On New Year's Eve, Mom made black-eyed peas.

"Eat 'em all," Dad said. "Every pea is a dollar we'll make this year."

I poured vinegar over mine and ate every last one.

CHAPTER 14

Flood

After the holidays, winter settled in to stay. It rained nonstop, which is all winter ever does. It seemed to fit everybody's moods, though. The gray clouds sat on us heavy with worry.

My arm twinged a lot where the break had been.

Sometimes it even kept me up at night.

It got so wet the ground couldn't hold any more rain and all the creeks in Coppertown started flooding. Peanut butter–colored water rushed through the erosion ditches and new streams popped up everywhere.

The phone rang late one school night, waking me from a deep sleep. I heard Mom answer down the hall. "Of course, Doris, he's welcome to stay. Do you need us to come get him? Okay. We'll see you in a bit."

She padded to my bedroom in her big fuzzy slippers.

"Jack, Mrs. Quinn is dropping Piran off in a few minutes. The flooding is getting pretty scary down there. Make room, okay?"

Dad, fully dressed, passed her in the hall. "I'm goin' down to see if I can help."

"I'll make coffee." Mom yawned.

We didn't get much sleep after that. I kept rubbing my arm and Piran worried all night.

"I should have grabbed my glove," he said again and again. "I can't believe I didn't grab my glove."

It rained throughout the night. My eyelids finally closed, heavy as cement, right before dawn. It seemed like I had just dozed off when the kitchen door closed. The sky was silver rather than charcoal, which is the only way I knew it was morning, but at least it wasn't raining. Piran and I stumbled to the kitchen and looked at my dad.

"Well?"

"It's up to the second stair on yu'uns back porch," he said, "but the water's not rising as fast now that the rain's stopped. We put about two hundred sandbags around the house, so I think you'll be okay." He looked exhausted. "Just pray it doesn't rain for a few days."

Piran fell heavily into a kitchen chair and sighed. "Thank you, Mr. Hicks."

"Oh, and your mom told me to give you this." He handed Piran his baseball glove, and Piran hugged it tight to his chest.

"Yu'uns still have to go to school," Mom said. "Go clean yourselves up and I'll make some breakfast."

I was so tired, I could barely swallow my oatmeal.

At school, we weren't the only ones running on no sleep. Most everybody was draggin'. Miss Post finally stopped her lesson. "Close your books, class. Today we're going to talk about erosion."

Which was really more talk about trees again. I may not have gotten it right about their roots holdin' the mine together, but their roots *would* hold the top layer of ground together. And when they died, they'd fall over and rot, creating organic soil for bugs, smaller plants, and animals to live in. It was hard to imagine trees were that important.

Without trees, without soil, the water had nowhere to go but into the earth, which in Coppertown was hard as a baked brick and didn't want it. That's why we had so much flooding.

The rain had stopped, but the water rose a few inches higher from runoff—now we understood why. We watched the Tohachee River out of our classroom window. It had turned into a swift-moving lake. The current carried all sorts of debris as it rushed by.

"I wonder whose porch swing that is," I said.

"I dunno, but I'm pretty sure that's my dad's ladder," Piran replied as we watched it tumble end over end, getting stuck once before it was pulled downstream again. If anybody had been standing nearby, it would've knocked 'em dead.

I was slow gathering my books at the end of the day and told Piran I'd catch up with him.

Once everybody was out of class, I approached Miss Post. "I thought that was real interestin', what you talked about today. Do you have any books about erosion, or nature, or…or trees?"

I'd never seen anybody smile that big. Miss Post loaded me up with two fat books and one that was a field guide entirely for plant identification. I couldn't believe there were so many different kinds of plants in the world and couldn't wait to learn about every single one.

"You keep 'em as long as you want, Jack, and let me know if you want more." She pressed her hands to her mouth and I couldn't help but notice a big ring sat on her finger where I didn't recall seein' one before.

It still rained after that, but not quite as heavy. The Tohachee River ran high, but stayed inside its banks. Things were so muddy, I was brown up to my knees most days. On the days it didn't rain, Piran and I walked downstream to see what we could find. It was spooky how high up things were left on the banks. A section of somebody's fence was even wedged into the rails of the bridge. Most of the washed-out debris was too busted or stuck to be of any use, but every now and then we'd find somethin' in okay shape. If we couldn't find who it belonged to, we kept it.

"I wish I had the pair to that boot," Piran said. "It was a good one, and it almost fit me."

"Mrs. Spokes sure was grateful to get her porch swing back," I said, remembering the hot apple cider she made for us.

"That was a pain in the butt to carry."

"It wasn't as bad as getting your dad's ladder out of the mud."

With the bad weather, I was stuck inside an awful lot. Things were so tense between my parents that it was the last place I wanted to be. I stopped watchin' TV in the den just to avoid them. Their silence hovered in the air like static electricity, and when they did talk, it was a thunderstorm. Mom was sure the mine was closed for good and that Dad should start looking for a job somewhere else. But Dad was convinced the Company would come around.

I was just tired of tiptoeing around them and eatin' beans for dinner. I swore if I ate one more bean, I would explode. My whole family had gotten quite musical, and I don't mean singin'.

I hung out at Piran's some, hoping to talk to Hannah. But she was always at a friend's house. The way Mrs. Quinn would say it, I didn't want to know *which* friend.

With the shorter days, neither one of us wanted to be walking home in the cold and dark, so I ended up spending most of my time reading in my bedroom, trying to block out the world.

Along with the book on plant identification, I studied books on insects, birds, and all the species of animals that should have been in Coppertown but weren't. I spent so much time reading that Miss Post had a hard time keeping up with me and ordered books from other libraries. She even found me a book about being a forest ranger.

A forest ranger—it was a real job!

I read that book over and over, dreaming of spending all my days hiking through forests, taking care of trees. The man who wrote it described how different the trunks felt, with their bumpy or smooth bark, and the spicy smell of sap, and the soft cushion of pine needles under his feet. It sounded like heaven to me.

CHAPTER 15

Ice Storm

I woke up one winter morning curled into a tight ball, my breath forming clouds in front of my face.

"It's freezing!" I said through chattering teeth.

"Ice storm, Jack. Power's out," Mom said as she shuffled down the hallway. "We need firewood. Get up." Since the TV was rarely on, we'd missed the alert on the nightly news.

I jumped from my bed to my dresser in one leap. Bouncing from foot to foot, I tried to keep them from touchin' the wooden floor, which was ice cold. I quickly grabbed a bunch of clothes and hopped back under the covers. After pulling on two sweatshirts, three pairs of socks, my gloves, and a hat—all crisp from the cold—I got out of bed.

I sat in my chair and pulled on my boots, which wasn't easy to do over the thick socks.

I jumped up and down and rubbed my arms as I headed toward the kitchen, trying to build up some body heat.

"Hurry up, Jack," Mom called from the kitchen.

"I'm coming!"

She turned on the gas oven. "This'll help some," she said. "Ray, can I turn on the water?" she yelled to Dad outside, where he was checking the pipes.

"Try it and we'll see," he called back.

She went to fill up the coffeepot, but as soon as she turned on the water, the house sounded like it was falling apart. Pipes rattled in the walls and water shot out from the cabinets underneath the sink.

"Turn it off! Turn it off!" she yelled through the window, then sopped up the water with the kitchen towel. "Jack, grab some towels from the linen closet."

I ran as fast as I could and handed her a stiff pile as Dad came in. "I hope to heck that's the only burst pipe we've got. I think I've got some spare in my metal shop."

"Phone's dead too," Mom said as I carefully climbed down the cement stairs outside. They were slick with ice and I could imagine slipping—my feet sliding out from under me—and bashing my head on the steps.

We can't have nice white fluffy snow here, no. Gotta have ice storms.

A frosty cloud drifted near my feet like it was too heavy to float any higher, and the ground was a solid sheet of ice. I looked up at our Red Hills, which had turned sparkly silver white, like wrinkled-up wrapping paper. Icicles hung from the power lines, the roof, the car, and the shed. My breath formed white puffs that lingered in the still air. Strangest of all, though, was that except for the snapping of icicles, it was unnaturally quiet. The few sounds there were didn't travel very far.

I walked slowly, slippin' across the frozen ground to the woodpile, and grabbed as many logs as I could hold. Dad bought a truckload from North Carolina every year. Lucky for us, he'd stocked up before the strike and before the Company took his truck back. Splinters snapped and echoed in that eerie stillness when I pulled their frozen edges apart. I couldn't hold very many logs and wished we still had the truck. We could've driven the firewood across the yard. It was the sort of day when Eli's Jeep would come in handy.

I shook my head. I didn't want anything that Eli had…except maybe Hannah.

With my arms full, I crunched back to the house.

Back inside, Dad crumpled newspaper and stuffed

it into the fireplace. We went through the entire Sunday edition and several matches before the wood finally took.

We dragged all the blankets from the beds and piled them up on the couch. Mom made hot chocolate with real milk—a treat since she couldn't use the water—and we burrowed in. Curled together like a basketful of puppies, we stared at the fire, waiting for the flames to chase away the cold.

"You think school's closed?" I asked.

"I'm gonna guess it is," Mom said. "But even if it isn't, I'm not gonna turn my son into a Popsicle. After you warm up, you and your dad can go see what's going on out there."

I stared at the flames jumping on the cold logs. "It's like the fire is dancin'," I said.

"Those are fire fairies," Mom said, nodding.

"Can you make a wish to 'em?"

"Couldn't hurt," she said and put her arm around me.

Usually I would have pulled away, but it felt nice. I made a wish for trees, and then leaned against her. Between the hot chocolate, the blankets, and the fire fairies, I soon fell asleep.

I awoke to a loud banging at the back door. "Hey, Jack," Piran called. "C'mon!"

I shuffled to the door rubbing my eyes. "What's up?" I asked.

"School's closed, and Killer Hill is covered with ice," he said. "Let's go sledding!"

"I don't have a sled!"

"Me neither, but a box works just fine." He held up a smashed piece of cardboard that had once held a washing machine or somethin' equally big. It was wet on one side. "I already tried it," he said. "It works great!"

"I think there are some boxes in my metal shop," Dad called from the den.

"Jack, make sure you're dressed warmly now," Mom hollered.

Couldn't dress much warmer, I thought as I layered on even more clothing. I felt like a walrus. "Aar! Aar!" I clapped my thick mittens together.

I waddled to the den and peeked around the corner before I left. Dad had his arm around Mom. I grinned—it had been a while since I'd seen them being sweet to each other. I didn't want to disturb them, so I quietly crept away.

"It sucks climbin' up," Piran gasped, sounding like his asthma was dangerously close to kicking in. "But it's great for sledding!" He leaped onto his box and careened down the hill yelling "Banzai!"

I jumped on my own box and followed suit. If I folded the front lip up, the makeshift sled worked pretty well.

We slid down dozens of times. Piran used his inhaler once after coughing some, but he pulled his ski mask over his nose to heat the air going into his lungs and refused to stop.

Then Eli showed up in his Jeep at the top of the hill. Even with his oversize tires, going down Killer Hill didn't seem like a good idea. But Hannah stepped out of Piran's house at the bottom bundled in a coat, hat, and gloves. I suppose that was all it took.

Eli gently stepped on the gas. The Jeep hadn't gone five feet before the ice took over and the car began to slide. Piran and I jumped out of the way. Eli's eyes were as big as his headlights as the Jeep slid past us and careened off the road. His tires hit a large rock, which almost knocked the top-heavy vehicle over. The impact sent a bag flying out the back of the Jeep, but it also set him back on the road. Eli straightened the tires and the Jeep kept sliding until it came to a gentle stop in front of the Quinns' house.

Piran went to grab whatever had flown out the back and ran it down to Eli. Eli didn't even thank him, just stuffed the bag angrily back into his Jeep.

Mr. Quinn came out of the house yelling, "This is no weather to be driving around in, young lady. You get back in here right now!" Hannah acted like she couldn't hear him over the loud stereo and climbed in the passenger side. They drove on down Lick Skillet Road with Mr. Quinn chasing behind, wavin' his fist 'til he realized he didn't have any shoes on.

I turned to Piran after his dad went back inside. "What was in the bag?"

With short breaths, he said, "Bunch of fluorescent light bulbs. Course, most of 'em were broken. What do you suppose he'd need with that many light bulbs?"

"I have no idea."

When we got back to our boxes, they had frozen to the ground, which might have been a good thing since Piran looked on the verge of a full-on asthma attack.

"It's a sign," I said. "Time for lunch."

We peeled up our sleds as best we could and split

up. I didn't envy Piran the mood in his house. Course, my mood had just been squashed too—Hannah was still crazy over Eli.

At home, Dad was busy with the pipe in the kitchen. Mom worked around him and heated me up some tomato soup with lots of pepper. It made me feel all warm inside and my mood improved some. Even with Hannah going off with Eli, how could I stay in a bad mood on a day off from school with sledding?

I grabbed a fresh box and ran back to Killer Hill. More kids were there now and even a few grown-ups.

Piran had taken some asthma medicine during lunch and seemed ready to go at it again. He invented a new sport he called bumper sledding. The whole trick was to knock each other off our sleds before we got to the bottom. We tore our boxes to shreds and ended up slidin' down on our bellies more than anything else. But we didn't care.

"Jack, you're soaking wet!" Mom said as I entered the kitchen and dripped on the floor. "Oh, I wish I could stick you in a hot bathtub."

"Did Dad fix the pipes?" I shivered.

"Yes, but we still don't have hot water."

"I'll go change, then."

"Oh no. You're not drippin' all over the house," she said. "Strip, young man."

"Mom! Well, turn around at least!"

"Sheesh!" She rolled her eyes and threw me a towel.

Naked and freezing, I ran to my bedroom and piled on more cold, crispy clothes, then ran back to the den and dove under the blankets on the couch to warm up.

Dad lit candles as the sun went down and grabbed two beers for him and Mom from the cooler outside. Then he straightened out a couple of wire coat hangers and we roasted hot dogs over the fire for dinner. The fat sizzled as it dripped on the logs and filled the room with a buttery smell. It was like camping in our own house.

"Grace, how about you tell us some Jack Tales," Dad said.

"Yeah!" I said.

Mom said I was named after my great-grandpa Jack Hicks, but I liked to imagine I was named after the hero of the old Appalachian stories. I loved the Jack Tales.

They had come over with our families from England, but turned into something really special when they reached our mountain home, most of all up on Beech Mountain where Mom and Aunt Livvy spent their summers growing up. Her grandma, my great-grandma Harmon, lived in an old log cabin without any power or running water, but Mom loved it up there anyhow.

Great-Grandma Harmon told the Jack Tales while Mom and Livvy shelled peas or shucked corn. They wouldn't stop as long as the stories didn't, so Great-Grandma told story after story, one leading into another.

Mom knew them all by heart and she told them in a thick mountain drawl.

My favorite was "Jack and the Robbers." It was about Jack, of course, and an ox, a donkey, a hound dog, a cat, and a rooster who all end up riding on top of each other like a pyramid. They come across the lair of some highway robbers and wait for 'em to return from thievin'. Jack and the animals scare them robbers so bad that they end up chasing 'em off—so they get to eat their vittles and keep their loot too!

Mom also told us "Jack and the Bean Tree"—the Appalachian version of "Jack and the Beanstalk"—and "Sop Doll," about a bunch of witches. Dad and I cheered and clapped when Mom was too tired to tell anymore.

Course, by then, we'd been listenin' to her hillbilly drawl so long that we were talking that way too, crackin' each other up.

"Let's jes set up a bed he'ar on the floor," Dad said.

"That's a right fine idea," Mom replied.

"I sure is tir'd," I said. "Ma, I got me a hankerin' to snack on some o' yer corn pone. They any left?"

"Law' no, I gave it to the pigs. They hain't had nothin' but leather britches and cornhusks since fall. I figgered to give 'em a treat."

"Well that were plum good of ye," I said. "But I sure is hungry. Maybe I'll go outside and chew on a tyre."

"You leave my wagon alone, y'hear?" Dad said. "It done nuthin' to ye."

We were in tears, laughing so hard. But all that talk of corn pone really did make me hungry, and Mom had some cornbread left over in the kitchen. I danced across the cold floor and raced back with a piece of cornbread, which I shoveled down too fast to taste.

It was too cold to sleep in our bedrooms, so we stoked the fire and piled the blankets and pillows into made-up beds on the floor. We'd just settled in to sleep when the power came back on. The whir of the heater smothered the sound of the crackling fire, and lights popped on like camera flashes.

I squinted and blinked against the sudden glare. Mom frowned.

Dad got up, turned off all the lights, turned the heat down, and came back to the den with a wide grin on his face. "Make some room fer yuh pa ther."

I fell asleep wishing things could stay just like this, happy and warm.

CHAPTER 16
Seeds

The miners stayed on strike through the rain, the ice, and the cold. They built a small shack just outside the main gate for when the weather got really bad and kept a fire going in a metal barrel to keep warm.

Every day, Dad returned home cold and depressed and went straight to his metal shop, where he made charms and model cars for Grandpa to display in his bait shop. Sometimes Grandpa would sell one to someone passing through and we'd have meat with dinner to celebrate.

Mom spent more and more of her time over at the Ledfords'. Mrs. Ledford's lung cancer had grown worse, and the miners' wives took turns helpin' out until somebody was there nearly round the clock. Sometimes I went with her, but I mostly just got in the way.

Being the only one in the house meant I answered the calls from the bill collectors. One day one of 'em yelled at me, "You're lying to me, son. I know your parents are home! Put your father on the phone right this minute!"

I hung up on him and leaned against the counter. *Don't cry, don't cry.* The phone rang again, but I ignored it as best I could.

We needed money. The stipend from the Union obviously wasn't enough. But what could I do to help my family? I felt so useless.

I asked Mom if I could get a job, but she said, "You have a job—to go to school and learn as much as you can."

That didn't stop me from lookin' around. But even the few part-time jobs were scooped up by out-of-work miners. I asked Grandpa if I could help in his store. He let me move boxes around on the weekends sometimes, but it was winter—his slow season. It wasn't nearly enough money to make a difference, and he couldn't afford to give me more.

I had to do *something.*

Watching my dad's shoulders sink lower and lower each day was driving me crazy. And I could have sworn his hair was turning gray.

About that time, Miss Post gave me a book on green-house gardening, which finally gave me an idea.

"Mom, do you have any leftover seeds from last year's garden?" I asked one night over yet another dinner of beans and rice.

All those summers in the mountains had turned her into a farmer, so every year she tried to grow a garden. It never worked. Farming in Coppertown was like working a man-made desert. But that didn't stop her tryin'.

"I could try to get the seeds started in paper cups and then they'd be ready to plant come spring," I said, then lowered my voice. "Since the Company hasn't been runnin', maybe they'd stand a chance this year. What do you think?"

Mom looked at me like she'd just found a lucky penny—heads up. "I think that's a *great* idea, Jack." She put down her fork and dove deep into the pantry. Dad and I exchanged a look, trying not to laugh. Our only view was of her rear end wiggling as she dug behind the last of the preserves on the bottom shelf.

She surfaced with several mason jars full of seed packets. "Ta-da!"

Mom and I went through them while Dad finished his dinner. Snow peas, carrots, collard greens, corn, tomatoes!

"They're old seeds, but some might work," she said. "By God, this family could use some vegetables."

Mom gave me a cookie sheet and I lined up small paper cups like I wanted the plants to be in the garden. With a permanent marker, I wrote on the sides what each one was going to be. Dad brought in some leftover manure and potting soil from last year's garden from the shed. I mixed them together and spooned a little into each cup, patting it down tightly.

"The carrot seeds are so tiny," I said as I punched a hole into the soil with my finger and sprinkled some in.

"I know," Mom said. "It's hard to believe those little things turn into big orange carrots, isn't it?"

"Hand me the corn and I'll get those going," Dad said.

When the cups were done I gently poured a little water over each one.

"Now, where to put them." Mom chewed on her lip. "They need to be right against a window for light."

"I know the place," I said. In my bedroom, I removed my baseball trophies and my cast from the top shelf of my bookcase. Mom laid down a kitchen towel and I put the cookie sheet on top.

"It still needs more light, though," Dad said. He

grabbed the swing-arm lamp from my desk and posi-
tioned it so it would shine right on the seed cups.

"Dad, I don't think regular light bulbs will work." I
frowned and flipped through my book. "Fluorescent lights
would work okay, but what we really need are grow lights."

"Hmm... I'll see what I can do about that," he said.
"But at least you've got a start."

We stood and looked at the little cups of dirt as if
they'd sprout right in front of us. As simple as those paper
cups were, they looked a little bit like hope.

I watered my seeds a tiny bit each day. Dad had added two
more lights from his metal shop with grow light bulbs he
bought at the hardware store way over in Murphy. My
bedroom turned into a mini lighthouse every day when
I switched them on before leaving for school. It made me
wonder about the light bulbs Eli'd had. Was he growing
somethin' too?

A few weeks later, while I was doing my homework,
something green flashed in the corner of my vision. I had
to stare close, but there it was, a tiny green thread poking
up through the soil. I ran to get my parents.

"Your babies are waking up!" Mom pointed at another cup. "Look, there's another one there."

"And there," Dad said and patted my back. "An artist and now you're a farmer too?"

"Gotta start somewhere." I smiled.

CHAPTER 17
Frog Eggs

E ventually winter wore itself out and spring crept in. The rain turned to thunderstorms. I could tell they were coming from the west because they rolled in over the smelters. Even sittin' unused, they made the air stink like rotten eggs.

Some nights I'd sit in bed and watch the light show on Tater Hill. The Company used the waste from copper mining to pave the parking lot up there, and the iron-rich slag attracted lightning like a magnet. I had a great view from my bedroom.

The storms still caused flooding, but they were farther apart now so it wasn't as bad. My arm ached a little less, and as February turned to March the days grew slightly longer. It had been gray for so long, I couldn't wait to leave my cave and go outside.

"Let's go exploring," I said to Piran one Sunday. I squinted at the bright glowing ball of sunshine that now lit the sky.

There wasn't much else to do. Baseball season had begun, but so many folks had moved away over the winter that we didn't have enough players to form an official team anymore. The Miners were finished. Turned out, the final game with the Rockets last spring had been my last.

Piran and I played catch, but it wasn't the same thing. *Swack, swack, swack*, we tossed the ball back and forth.

"I wish I could go back and warn myself that baseball was dead," I said.

"What would you say?" Piran asked. "Enjoy it while it lasts? Too bad, so sad?"

"I dunno." I frowned. It was rotten news, no matter when I learned it. "Let's do something else."

We were about restless enough to walk the entire Appalachian mountain chain, so we followed the railroad tracks upstream. Before we knew it we were cutting north to the Old Number 2 Tailings Pond. We hadn't even agreed to go there. It was like our feet were in charge.

"Whoa," Piran said as it came into view.

"Unbelievable." I gaped.

The tailings pond had flooded over the winter, forming an actual lake. I don't know what was stranger looking, its usual weird appearance or seein' it look like something sort of normal.

We hiked around to the northeast side. The river had flooded so much that there were several new feeder creeks cutting through to the main pond.

"Think it'll stay this way?" Piran asked. "We could get a boat and water-ski."

"I bet when things dry up this summer, the pond will be cut off again," I said, staring into the shallow water. Something caught my eye floating just under the surface. "What are those?"

Clinging to a branch stuck in the mud were dozens of clear slimy balls with little black dots inside.

I leaned down to get a better look. "No way."

"What?"

"Those are frog eggs!"

"What? Where?" Piran asked.

"See those little balls, they kinda look like jelly?" I pointed. "Remember we studied them in school?"

Piran looked at me like I had three heads.

"Well, I do anyhow, and those are definitely frog eggs."

Back in town, as we walked by the closed Company store, Piran stopped so suddenly, I bumped right into him. "Hey, what the…"

I wished I hadn't seen what he'd stopped for. Hannah was making out with Eli Munroe next to the loading docks. She was pressed up against him with her arms thrown over his shoulders. His hands were on her…

"My dad is about ready to kill her for going out with that moron," Piran said. "It's been like World War Three in my house lately."

"How come she can't see what an idiot he is?" I frowned. "I mean, the guy is five bricks shy of a load."

Just then Hannah noticed us standing there. She stared right at me as she took a drag from a strange, skinny cigarette and kept kissing Eli. Heat rose up from the soles of my feet and spread all over my body. Anger, disgust, or embarrassment—I wasn't sure. I had to look away.

Piran and I sulked home. Neither one of us spoke, but probably for different reasons.

CHAPTER 18
Garden

H appy birthday, Jack!" Mom said as she came into my room and gave me a big, sloppy kiss on my forehead before I could stop her. "Fourteen, I can't believe it! You're gettin' so big."

"Ugh!" I complained but smiled anyway.

She looked at my seedlings and rubbed a leaf carefully between her fingers. With constant light and water, they'd grown several inches tall—my own mini-forest.

"Jack, I know it's your birthday and a Saturday and all, and you can do anything you want today, but I think it's time to transfer these to the garden. Would you like to do that this morning?"

"Yeah!" I smiled and hopped out of bed.

"We'll just need to get the garden ready first," she said.

After breakfast, we grabbed two shovels from Dad's

metal shop and walked out to the small fence that ran along one side of the garden in the backyard.

"We need to turn the soil, loosen it up so the roots will have an easier time spreading out," Mom said. "Watch how I do it." She stuck her spade into the ground and jumped on the head with her feet on either side of the handle. It sank easily into the earth. Then she leaned back on the handle, scooped up a big chunk of soil, and flipped it over into the hole she'd just created.

"Not bad," she said. "It shouldn't be too hard to turn."

I tried to jump on my shovel but landed on my rear end instead. "Ow!"

"Try it again." Mom laughed. "I fell the first time I jumped on a shovel too."

Three more tries and I finally landed squarely on the head. I fought to keep my balance as the spade slid into the ground beneath me. It was kind of like a little amusement ride. Once I'd gotten the shovel blade deep enough, I levered the handle like Mom had, but I couldn't fill my shovel as full as hers for nothing. I had no idea she was so strong.

Once I dug too far outside the garden and scraped up red clay, completely different from the garden's black soil and hard as a brick. "Hey, Mom, look."

"Yup. You can tell where I've been working cow

manure into the ground for years now, can't ya? The darker soil is full of nutrients for your little seedlings, like a gourmet meal. The red ground is dead."

The garden wasn't very big, but it was hard work. *How much work would it take to change all the ground in Coppertown?*

After we raked the soil into even rows, the garden was ready. I ran to get my seedlings, but then walked out slowly with them like I was carryin' china. I set them down and then took a deep breath—a clean breath. Without the Company running, the air didn't have that acrid smell to it anymore. I smiled. My seedlings might have a fighting chance.

We lined up the cups in the same order they were on my cookie sheet, setting them on top of the dirt rows. They looked much smaller spread apart and I tried to imagine how they'd fill in as they grew larger—at least I hoped they would.

I carefully turned each seedling over, loosened the cup off its roots, and then turned the plant into a small hole I dug with my hand. They were so delicate—each one a small treasure waiting to transform into somethin' grand.

We slid the seed packets over bent hangers, which we stuck in the ground at the end of each row to remind us what was what.

Then I dragged the hose from the house. Mom put a special showerhead on the nozzle that she'd been using all the years the garden never made it. Sunlight reflected on the water beads like stars as I sprayed a gentle arc from side to side, back and forth over the tiny seedlings and dark soil. Back and forth, back and forth. The soil turned black as it absorbed the water—like the ground was supposed to do in Coppertown but didn't.

I imagined I was one of the seedlings stretching up to the water and the warm sun. Were they humming with joy? I could almost hear 'em. I smiled at the idea that I could bring things to life like that.

"How long before they take off, do you think?" I asked Mom as we stood back to admire our work.

"I'd give 'em a few weeks to settle in and get going," Mom said. "You'll need to water them every day, okay? Just like you been doin'—it's your job."

"Yes, ma'am!" I nodded.

Dad leaned in the doorframe. "They're outside planting Jack's garden," he said into the phone receiver, the cord stretched across the kitchen.

I looked at Mom. It had always been *her* garden. Would she mind the slip? Obviously not. She shot me a huge smile.

"Grace," Dad shouted. "Your dad wants to know what time he should come over for Jack's birthday dinner."

"Tell him five o'clock and that we're having macaroni and cheese, Jack's favorite." She turned to me. "And we're having Mrs. Markley's chocolate cake too."

"Oh yum!" It was a tradition in our family, a recipe from way back, and it was the best chocolate cake on the planet. For all our slim meals of late, I was going to eat like a king that evening!

"You did good work, Jack. Hand me the hose and I'll finish up watering. Go find Piran and be home in time for your birthday dinner."

My birthday dinner.

I knew Mom and Dad still couldn't do much in the way of presents, but I wondered what Grandpa would give me. Maybe Mom had told him about the dirt bike? A voice whispered in the back of my mind that he couldn't afford it either, but I ignored it. Dreamin' was free!

When I got home from hanging out with Piran (who gave me a baseball card with bubblegum that he bought himself at Dilbeck's Pharmacy), Grandpa's truck was pulled up out front of the house with a tree—an entire tree, roots and all—standing up in a bucket in his truck bed with a blue bow tied around its trunk.

I barely had time to hide my disappointment.

"Happy birthday, Jack!" Grandpa said as he strode out to the yard. "What do you think? Grace told me about yer garden, and with that art you did for me at Christmas, I figured this'd be the perfect thing to get ya. It's a dogwood tree. I dug it up from the woods outside Coppertown. You can start that forest of yours."

Not a bike, a tree. A tree that Grandpa dug up himself?

And from the size of it, that was no easy task.

I looked at my grandpa—really looked. When did he stop standing up straight? Was he hurting? I couldn't believe he'd dug up an entire tree for me.

"You think it'll live?" I asked, suddenly anxious.

"I think it's got a better chance than it ever might've before. And I think it has a better chance with you."

I didn't know what to say. My eyes got all watery and I hugged Grandpa so tight.

Finally he grunted and I stepped back. "Oh, I'm sorry! Did I hurt your back?"

"Not to worry, Jack," he said. "That was just my heart bustin' its seams."

I used some of the leftover manure from the garden and dug a hole nearby for the tree.

Grandpa was impressed with my hole-diggin' skills, which I had to put to work on the red ground. That ground was much tougher and before long I had blisters on my hands, but I had to finish. Mom stuck some bandages on me and Dad gave me some gloves to wear. I turned manure into the ground for a long time, knowing that what I did might make the difference between the tree living or dying.

When it was finally planted in the ground, it seemed much shorter. Of course, a good portion of the tree was underground, waitin' to take root. It's trunk looked skinnier too with all that bare land behind it, humbling it. Like David taking on Goliath, it needed me to keep it safe in the harsh environment of Coppertown. It needed *us*.

I handed Grandpa the hose to water it. "It'll be *our* forest," I said.

CHAPTER 19
Jobs

April was more of the same old, same old. I thought I was gonna melt with boredom. I couldn't wait for May and the return of Music Fridays.

Aunt Livvy, Uncle Bubba, and Buster came over to join in since it was the first music night of the season and they didn't have anything like that in Lumpkin.

Aunt Livvy went on about how much I'd grown, but all I could see was how much my dad had shrunk. When he stood next to Uncle Bubba, it was obvious how much weight he'd lost. He used to be the bigger of the two, but not anymore.

I acted like I couldn't overhear Mom and Aunt Livvy talking about it as I grabbed an RC Cola from Grandpa's cooler.

"He won't give up on it, Livvy," Mom whispered. "I don't know what to do."

"Have you thought about gettin' a job?" Livvy said.

"I got married straight out of school." Mom laughed. "I don't know about anything other than being a wife and mother."

"Desperate times deserve desperate measures, Grace."

Buster, Piran, and I tried to talk baseball, but it just got us down. Besides, it was hard to concentrate with the group of girls from our class looking at us and gigglin' every five minutes.

Buster checked his shirt. "Did I spill somethin'?"

"Nah, yer fine," Piran said. "Do I have something in my teeth?"

I rolled my eyes. "Piran, Beth Ann has a crush on you. Didn't you know?"

Buster smacked Piran's arm. "Go, Mr. Studly!"

"She does?" Piran turned red from his neck right up to the top of his shiny red ears. Buster and I died laughing as we headed to the water's edge.

We skipped stones like we used to, teasing Piran about Beth Ann and comparing our favorite sports stars. It all felt so familiar, and yet everything was different.

My parents got into a heated conversation that night. Even with their door closed, I could tell it had something to do with what Aunt Livvy had said at the park. They got louder and louder until their bedroom door opened with a *whoosh* then slammed shut. Dad stomped down the hall, past my bedroom to the den.

I had a hard time getting to sleep, and when I finally did, I tossed and turned all night.

Mom was already gone the next morning when I entered the kitchen. The newspaper was pulled apart and scattered all over the table, where Dad sat staring at his hands. I peeked in the den. A pillow and blanket were rumpled on the couch.

"Where's Mom?" I asked.

"She's off to find a *job*," Dad muttered.

I made myself a bowl of cereal and tried to be quiet about it. Halfway through my meal, Dad suddenly pushed his chair back and stalked out to his metal shop.

When I returned home from hangin' out with Piran, Mom was sitting in the car in front of the house. I couldn't tell how long she'd been there, but the hood was cold and already covered with a thin sheen of silicone dust when

I touched it to get her attention. She wiped her eyes before she climbed out. She looked so tired and small as I opened the kitchen door for her.

Dad was waiting inside. He had to know she'd been sittin' in out there. He would have heard her pull up. "I gather it didn't go well?"

Mom glared at him then sank into a kitchen chair. "Fifteen women showed up for the same job," she said. "I didn't stand a chance."

Dad turned to the sink before I could read his expression. Sitting there in her Sunday dress and heels, she looked so fragile. "They made a mistake," I said. *Who had the nerve to turn away my mom?*

She blinked, but didn't look up. "I'll go change and get dinner going."

CHAPTER 20

Hannah

T hings were going downhill at Piran's house too.

"I can come over," I told Piran on the phone the next weekend. Another storm had hit, trapping us indoors. Maybe, just maybe, Hannah would be home for once.

"Nah, I'll come up there," he replied, then whispered into the receiver, "I need to get outta here."

"Why, what's up?"

"I'll tell ya when I get there."

We sat in my room going through old magazines, but I could tell Piran wasn't paying much attention. He kept chewing his nails and staring at the floor.

I waited for him and kept peeking at him out of the corner of my eye.

Finally he spit it out in a rush. "Hannah's pregnant."

"What?" My stomach turned upside down.

"She broke the news last night." He didn't look up. "She and Eli are getting married."

"Married! But... But she's in high school! And... And he doesn't even have a job!"

"She graduates next month, and she's the same age my mom was when she married my dad," Piran said. "But, God! Eli Munroe is going to be my brother-in-law!"

My tomato soup lunch threatened to come back up. I'd been holding out hope that Hannah would realize how wrong Eli was for her. I'd been waiting for my chance to show her how right *I* was for her. But now it didn't matter.

Married.

"They're moving into an apartment in town," Piran said. "My parents are furious."

Piran's face was splotchy red and slack. I don't think I'd ever seen him so upset.

"I'm real sorry, Piran," I muttered as my heart sank down to my toes.

"Yeah."

Hannah and Eli were married at the courthouse two weeks later. Only immediate family attended, so Piran told me what happened—even though I wasn't sure I wanted to hear.

"Hannah was all googly-eyed, but Eli looked like he'd swallowed a toad. He was green I tell ya—*green*! Everybody was frownin' and grumbling like right before a fight breaks out. I thought my dad and Eli's dad were gonna come to blows, because Mr. and Mrs. Munroe blamed Hannah, of course. Like she got pregnant on purpose or somethin'. It was the most depressing wedding I've ever been to."

Hannah and Eli didn't go on a honeymoon, just hung out in Eli's apartment—their apartment. I tried so hard not to think about it, but it kept creepin' into my brain.

As if that wasn't bad enough, the Rockets baseball team was all over the newspaper as they soaked up win after win. *If the Miners were playing, it would be us in those papers.*

My heart was as bare as Coppertown, and I didn't think I could sink any lower.

CHAPTER 21
Tadpoles

Without being wrapped up in baseball season, Piran and I didn't know what to do with ourselves.

"We could go swimmin' in the sinkhole," Piran suggested one weekend.

"God, Piran, that's the sort of creepy thing Buster would come up with," I complained. "You know my grandpa died in that collapse before it filled up with water. That would be like swimming around in his grave. Besides, there's still equipment down there, and you can't get in anyhow."

"Half the fence is rotted," Piran said. "The runoff water ate up the bottom of the metal posts. I knocked one over the other day without barely pushing at all. C'mon, I dare you."

I gave him a dirty look. "You know what happened the last time I took one of your dares, Piran Quinn. I don't need no more broken bones," I said. "How about we go check on the frog eggs up at the tailings pond?"

"We're not supposed to go there neither," Piran reminded me.

"Nothing is gonna keep me away from those frog eggs," I said.

On the way past the trestle bridge, Piran looked at me sideways. "I have an idea," he said. When he walked out to the center of the bridge, my jaw dropped.

"Don't worry, the train don't run no more. C'mon!" He unzipped his pants and peed into the mud below. "It seems only fittin', don't ya think?"

I nodded and walked out to join him, taking the awkwardly spaced beams step by step. That day in August came back to me in a rush and my knees grew weak.

Piran urged me on. "C'mon, Jack, you can do it."

Soon I was by his side and doing the same thing. The bumpy landscape of Coppertown spread out in front of me as I let go with a record-breaking pee onto the exact spot where I'd broken my arm. It did feel like a good payback as I replaced the bad memory of lying in that ditch in pain with the new one of doing something goofy with my best friend.

The tailings pond was starting to dry up. The feeder creeks were down to a trickle and several small ponds were now completely cut off from the main pond.

"I was afraid of that," I said. "I'll bet these are all gone by summer."

"Hey, look!" Piran pointed at where the eggs had been. Tiny black tadpoles, no bigger than macaroni, wiggled through the water.

We stretched across the ground to get a better look.

Down low, I noticed something else—green reeds were sproutin' out of the ground all around the ponds. Some even had the beginnings of leaves on them.

I shouted with excitement. "Piran, look—weeds!"

"Oh yeah," he replied with much less enthusiasm.

"It's nature, Piran," I tried to explain. "After a hundred years of nothing, *nothing*, nature is comin' back to Coppertown!"

"Eh. I like Coppertown the way it is," Piran said. "What do you want a bunch of weeds around for anyway? I'd probably just be allergic, which would make my asthma worse."

I was speechless. How could my best friend not understand? Even so, he didn't dampen my mood. Weeds! Trees couldn't be far behind.

I smiled all the way home as I stared at the ground lookin' for more signs of life moving in. How long would it take for *everything* to turn green?

I told Miss Post about the tadpoles, although I didn't tell her where I'd found 'em.

"Jack, honey," she said, "we don't have frogs in Coppertown."

"The eggs must've come down with the flood waters or something, because they're here all right," I said. "There's weeds growing along the banks too."

She wasn't convinced but found me an entire book on amphibians anyway. It went into way more detail than our school science book. I read about the stages they went through, called metamorphosis, from eggs to tadpoles to frogs, and learned that frogs actually breathe through their skin.

I can't wait to see that!

According to the book, the tadpoles still had over a month to go before they'd be bona fide frogs. Would the pond last that long for them?

I pulled out the book Miss Post got me earlier in the year on plant identification. How cool to actually have living examples to compare to the pictures in the book! I walked all over Coppertown with that book sticking out my back pocket or my nose stuck in it studying.

I didn't recognize most of the weeds popping up everywhere, but I picked out the kudzu right away. Whenever we drove outside of Coppertown, we passed miles of land swallowed up entirely by the green vines. It was pretty in its way, but a little scary too. Though I'd never thought of nature as being aggressive, kudzu was proof of it.

CHAPTER 22

Security Guards

That weekend, Mom called me over to the garden. "Jack, see how long the pea plants are getting? We need to make a lattice for them to climb up!"

"How we gonna do that?"

"I'm not sure. They never got this far before." Mom tapped her chin. "I know!"

We got some rebar from Dad's metal shop, stuck it deep into the ground at each end of the row of peas, and ran kitchen string between 'em. Then we gently curled the tendrils around the strings, givin' the vines something to grab on to.

We were just finishing up when Dad sped into the yard, kicking up gravel as he screeched to a stop. His face was red as a beet as he slammed his car door and stormed into the house. Mom and I looked at each other warily and followed him in. Dad paced back and forth in the kitchen like a mad bull.

"The Company's brought in security guards from out of town," he said through gritted teeth, all the veins sticking out on his neck and forehead. "They never did anything so low down before."

"I don't understand. Why would they need security guards if the Company is closed?" Mom asked.

"I don't know, Grace, but it can't be good," Dad said. "They're planning something."

He said they were dressed all in black like some sort of special military unit, although that's not what they were. They were sent in to intimidate the strikers, mess with the picket line, bust up the Union.

Grandpa Chase showed up right before dinner, mad as a stuck pig. "I don't believe this. Workers have been strikin' for years. We always came up with an agreement everybody could live with," he said. "On the way over here, I heard that one of those security guards followed Tom Hill home and cursed at him in his own front yard. Sheriff Elder couldn't even arrest the jerk—said the guy was on public property when he did it. What has the world come to?" He shook his head. "Security guards my foot. They're bullies with badges."

"Want dinner, Pa?" Mom asked. "It's nothing fancy, but I'm sure we could make it stretch."

I looked at the pot on the stove and swallowed—beans and rice again, and so little that it was hard to imagine us dividing it with one more person. I could have eaten the whole amount all by myself.

"Thanks, Grace, but I can't stay," Grandpa said, and I sighed with relief. "Just wanted to make sure yu'uns knew what was going on."

CHAPTER 23
Eavesdropping

S chool let out the next week, but I hardly cared.

"Have a good summer," Miss Post said with a sigh as people started leaving the room.

I gave her back the library books she'd given me as well as the book on plant identification, but she handed that one back. "You keep this one, Jack. It was my copy."

"Oh, oh, I couldn't."

But she pushed it back toward me. "I think you need this book more than I do."

"Thank you, ma'am," I said. But even as grateful as I was, I couldn't smile. "Miss Post, are you getting married? Are you gonna leave?"

"Oh, Jack." Her eyes filled with tears and she nodded.

I don't know what came over me, but I hugged her tight as can be, right around her middle—we were nearly the same height. If anybody saw, they might have laughed at me, but right then, I didn't care a wit. "I'm gonna miss you."

She squeezed me back. "I'm going to miss you too. You never stop reading, y'hear?"

"What is it with you and older women?" Piran teased as we left the building. He'd seen me after all.

I just smiled. "Can I help it if they find me attractive?"

He rolled his eyes and pushed me. "Want to go for ice cream?"

"Nah." I didn't want to admit I couldn't afford it.

"I can buy," he said. "You've treated me plenty."

Somethin' inside me just couldn't say yes. I wondered if that's how Piran felt when I used to help him out. It was a hard lump to swallow, pride. "Thanks, but I gotta get home."

"Fishin' tomorrow, then?" Piran asked.

"Okay, I'll see you in the mornin.'"

But we didn't get to fish. News came that afternoon that Mrs. Ledford had finally passed. The viewing was the next day.

Mom made a cornbread casserole for the reception afterward at the Ledfords' house. We all dressed in our Sunday best and headed for the Methodist church. "You look pretty, Mom."

"Thank you, Jack," she replied and tugged at my too-short sleeves. "You look right handsome yourself."

"Jacket could be a bit bigger." My shoulders were pulled behind me like chicken wings.

"You're getting so tall," she said and hugged me. Engulfed by the smell of Ivory soap and cornbread, I kept myself scrunched up so my jacket wouldn't rip apart at the seams. Finally she turned away, wiping tears from her eyes. I held her hand tightly as we walked into church.

It was much more modest than our Episcopal church—just a white box with a pointy roof that was packed solid with people. Folks squeezed into the pews and stood against the walls.

We got in line to view the body. I hated open caskets. Mrs. Ledford looked so tiny and kind of silly in the rouge and lipstick I knew she never wore. She had on her purple dress, the one with the big pink flowers. I'd seen it on her many times under better circumstances.

Mom placed her hand on Mrs. Ledford's and whispered with a sniff, "Rest in peace, Helen."

Dad found some seats for Mom and me at the back of the church and went to stand against the wall with the other men. Even Crazy Coote, wearing an old suit with his hair slicked back, was there. He looked right at me with that intense stare of his before I turned away.

Pastor Raht talked about Mrs. Ledford being in a better place with her Lord and not having to suffer anymore. Watching Mr. Ledford through the tangle of shoulders and stiff hair, I wondered if the preacher's words made him feel any better.

It seemed like everybody in town wanted to stand up and say somethin' about Mrs. Ledford. After a while, I had a hard time keeping still. I looked around at all the familiar faces. Without smiles, everybody looked tired and old. Nobody looked right in their Sunday suits— too tight here, too short there. They fiddled with their collars and pulled at their ties, ready to throw on overalls the minute they got home. That's what I planned to do anyhow.

I twisted around and stared at the big hole high on

the wall above the church entrance. It was about three feet wide, like a round window but without glass.

"Mom, what's that?" I whispered, pointing quickly.

"It's called a spirit hole. It's there so Mrs. Ledford's soul can float out to Heaven," she replied.

"Is it always open like that?"

"Yes, shhh."

"Even when it rains or snows?"

"Yes, Jack. Now hush."

I spent the rest of the sermon trying to catch a glimpse of Mrs. Ledford heading out that spirit hole as a winged angel, or maybe a misty ghost. I wasn't sure what she'd look like, so I stared hard—I didn't want to miss her.

We went to the Ledfords' house after the funeral. Mom wedged her casserole onto the dining-room table already overflowing with cookies, sandwiches, and more casseroles, then joined the other wives in the kitchen. Dad talked in the corner with his fellow strikers, their faces grim. There wasn't much for Piran and me to do except stand around and listen to gossip.

Even at fourteen, we were still young enough, I

guess, that people didn't think nothin' about saying stuff around us. Unfortunately, I ended up next to the old biddies—three miners' wives who liked to get everybody in trouble.

"I heard that Nat Faysal crossed the picket line to talk to those guards yesterday."

"He did not. That's not true."

"My son's wife's sister saw him with her own eyes."

"Whatever for, though? Why would he do it?"

"Who knows. Maybe he was trying to put in a word for his son—get him a job?"

"Well! That does it. I will never shop at Faysal's again! I won't support no strikebuster."

"Me neither."

Father Huckabay interrupted them. "Ladies, my ears were buzzing with your wicked gossip. True or not, do you really think this appropriate conversation for a funeral?"

Good for him! I hid my grin.

The women looked at the floor and at each other, then broke up and found other ears to burn.

I kept getting jostled as people passed me to get to the food or the kitchen. I backed up against a wall and ended up around a corner from Sheriff Elder. His conversation with his deputy was much more interesting.

"...found a field over in Cherokee County. They set up cameras and got enough evidence to bust a small growing ring—only five guys, but over a million dollars' worth of marijuana. We're gonna start a helicopter flyover here in Polk County as soon as the budget gets approved. We'll be able to spot growin' fields much easier from above, though we've already got two we're closing in on. That one in Hell's Holler and another in Devil's Den. Got cameras on 'em both—just waitin' for enough evidence."

"Jack, come help with this," Mom said. I spun around, but not before Sheriff Elder caught my eye and frowned.

Mom handed me a large glass bowl full of red punch. "Careful now."

I turned around slowly, trying to keep it from sloshing.

"Where should I put it?" I asked. Between all the CorningWare casserole dishes, slabs of meat, and mystery dishes still covered in tinfoil, there wasn't a bare surface anywhere.

"Just find a spot," she said as she waved her hand and returned to the kitchen.

"Right," I said and rolled my eyes.

I slowly moved to the doorway of the living room, without spilling, but still couldn't see a good place to put the punch bowl.

Suddenly, across the room, Mr. Ledford slumped over like Jell-O.

"Help him lie down. Give him some air!" everybody started yelling at once. "Call an ambulance!"

Somebody rushed by me, knockin' the punch bowl right out of my arms. Red juice splashed everywhere and soaked into Mrs. Ledford's white carpet.

"I'm sorry!" I cried to my mom, who was suddenly by my side with a towel and some club soda. My nose swelled and hot tears ran down my face.

"I've got it, Jack."

I caught a glimpse of Mr. Ledford through the paisley dresses and navy pants. He was so pale, he matched the carpet he was lying on.

"Will he be okay?" I sobbed. Months of tension burst out of me in a flood. I was red with embarrassment, but I couldn't stop.

"I'm sure he'll be fine," she replied as she kneeled down, poured the club soda on the carpet, and scrubbed with the towel. "The ambulance will be here soon." She looked up at me, her face wrinkled with concern. "Find

Piran and yu'uns just go on, okay?" she said. "Be home before dark."

I wiped my nose down my coat sleeve and rubbed the tears from my eyes. When I looked up, Hannah was staring right at me with a crinkled forehead and her pink lips forming a perfect O. Was that disgust or understanding on her face? I couldn't tell. And even though she looked more beautiful than ever, I squinted my eyes at her—she wasn't one to judge, and it was a little late for her to care. I pushed my way through the kitchen and out the back door.

Piran was already outside. "It was too stuffy in there," he said. "What's all the racket?"

"Mr. Ledford fainted," I told him and looked down so he wouldn't see I'd been cryin'. "They called an ambulance."

We could already hear its siren leaving the hospital in the distance.

"Let's get out of here," I said. I pulled off my jacket, shoes, and socks.

I ran down the road, the dirt warm under my bare feet. The wind dried my tears as I left Piran behind. At the bridge, I grabbed the rail and slipped my legs over the edge, letting my feet wave high above the water. I threw rocks as hard as I could, determined to break the river in half.

"That sucked," Piran said when he finally caught up with me. He gasped a few times before he sat. "What was that about?"

"Sorry," I muttered. "I'm just sick of funerals." I threw a big rock. *Kaplunk!* "What a rotten start to summer."

I was tired. Tired of money being so tight. Tired of my parents arguin' and all the tension at home. Tired of my friends moving away and seeing FOR SALE signs on the stores in town. I wanted things back to normal.

But no, not that either, I thought. I didn't want my dad back in the mines, not ever. I felt like my face was gonna stick in a permanent frown—things were all wrong.

Piran and I stared at the water for a long time.

A tiny blue shape gently left the shadow of the bridge and floated with the current into the sunlight.

What is that? I wondered. It looked like a little cup except for its ragged, sharp edge. The inside was white and the outside was a soft blue with brown spots.

I gasped and pointed. "It's a bird's egg!"

"No way," Piran said. "Where would it come from?"

"Somewhere upstream, I suppose."

I watched it bob on the water's surface until it was out of sight.

CHAPTER 24

Fishing

I was going to meet Piran the next day to go fishing, which meant hiking way far south to get to where the fish could live. I checked my garden before I left. A green mass of leaves covered the string lattice with little white flowers and a few leaves that looked like...

"Mom, Mom!" I shouted as I ran inside. "Come look!"

She followed me out to the garden and I pointed to the fatter of the green leaves. "What are those?"

"Jack! You've grown sugar snap peas!" She hugged me and tried to swing me around but couldn't lift me up. Instead, we ended up dancing in a circle like we'd lost our minds.

"So now what?" I asked as I stopped to catch my breath.

She plucked one of the pods off the vine and handed

it to me. "You eat it!" Then she broke off another and took a bite out of hers. "Mmm. It's so sweet! Try one."

"Raw?" I made a face.

"Yes, raw. It's good."

I nibbled at the end of my snap pea. It crunched cool and sweet in my mouth, still wet with dew.

"Hey, that's not bad," I said and pulled another one off.

We smiled as we munched on the green pods until there weren't any left.

"Oh no, I'm sorry!" I said mid-chew. "Did you want these for dinner?"

Mom laughed. "Y'know, when I used to visit my grandma up on Beech Mountain, the sugar snap peas never made it out of her garden either."

She squinted at me. "Jack, it's time for your summer haircut. Let me grab my trimmers."

"Nawww, Mom! Piran's waitin' for me."

"This'll only take a minute."

I kicked at the ground as she went inside. I hated having my head shaved, but Mom did it every summer. "It's easier to clean you up," she said when she came back. "And it's cooler."

"Then why don't you shave your head?" I mumbled.

"Here we go." She pulled the extension cord after her. "Lean over."

As I did, sunlight fluttered in the corner of my eye and I looked up quick. No way. Was that a...a bird? Nothing was there. Besides, there hadn't been a bird in Coppertown for a hundred years. I had to be dreamin'.

Mom clicked the button and the trimmers whined to life, sounding too much like the saw Dr. Davis had used to remove my cast. As she buzzed across my head I winced and watched my hair fall to the ground at my feet.

A short time later I walked to the bridge with my new fishing rod over my shoulder. I rubbed my stubbly head. It felt so strange and naked. Then I burst out laughing when I saw Piran. He was bald too.

"My mom said it's so she can find ticks easier," Piran complained as we walked toward the Bait 'n Beer. "But I ask you, when was the last time anybody ever saw a tick in these parts?"

Grandpa's store sat by Old Brawling Town Creek, a feeder creek for the Tohachee. It was called Old Brawling because a lot of fights used to break out down that way

when the first miners came over. They hadn't just come from Cornwall, England, but also from Germany, Italy, Greece, and even as far away as Lebanon. There were a few Black townsfolk too, but they weren't miners. Grandpa Chase said they were superstitious about going underground. They may have been the smartest of the bunch for thinkin' that way.

Not all those folks got along so well at first. Back then Coppertown was like livin' in the Wild West. Grandpa told great stories about it—like the one about the man who was shot for cheatin' at cards, but nobody knew who he was. So the coroner had him embalmed and they propped him up in a casket in the window of the hardware store so some passersby might identify him. Crazy.

Bells rang as we entered Grandpa's store, which was filled with the *chirp, chirp* of live bait. He got one glimpse of our cue-ball heads and laughed 'til I worried he might choke.

"It's not funny!" I said. "You're lucky she can't get a hold of you."

Grandpa rubbed the top of his head. "Not much left for her to shave off anyhow. What yu'uns up to today?"

"Goin' fishin'," Piran said.

"You gonna walk all that way?" Grandpa asked.

"It's only 'bout an hour upstream," I said. Fish didn't live downstream from the Company, and it took a while to get to 'em even on the upstream side. But it was one of the only places in Coppertown that had plants—a little kudzu and broom sage, which I found in my plant identification book—not much, but more than I was used to seein'. Being upwind of the smelters made all the difference. Someday I'd have a car to get there and it wouldn't seem so far, although I didn't really mind the walk.

"Well, you want crickets or worms?" Grandpa asked.

"Worms'll be fine," I said.

"Go get yourselves a cupful," Grandpa said.

Piran held the cup while I dug through the dirt bin with my hands.

"You not gonna use the scoop?" Piran asked.

"Nah, I like to feel them wigglin' around my fingers," I said. "Besides, I get more worms than dirt this way."

I set the cup on the counter right next to a new jar full of strange, gnarled shapes. "What's that, Grandpa?"

"That there's pickled ginseng," he said. "Did you know your great-grandfather was a 'sang' hunter? He made good money selling it to Chinese merchants."

"Hunt it?" Piran asked. "Is it some kind of animal?"

"Naw," Grandpa said, laughing. "It's a root. It's supposed to be a cure for just about anything."

"I guess Mrs. Ledford didn't use it, then," I said.

Grandpa replied quietly, "Nothing can cure lung cancer, Jack."

I blushed, remembering Grandma Chase. "I'm sorry…" I mumbled.

"People pay money for it?" Piran asked. "Maybe we could hunt sang. Where do we get it?"

"Well now, that's the big secret, ain't it?" Grandpa leaned across the counter and whispered, "It's very hard to find, and sang hunters are highly protective of their growin' patches. Nowadays it's grown commercially, like this here jar, but back in the day, it was a big deal. Sometimes men got shot over it."

"Like pot fields," Piran said.

"How do you know about that?" Grandpa leaned back with a frown.

"I just heard, is all." Piran glanced at me and the tops of his ears turned red. I'd told him what I'd overheard Sheriff Elder say at the Ledfords' house after the funeral.

"Maybe we should just stick to fishin'," I said, and Piran nodded in agreement.

I pushed an escaping worm back into the cup and dug for change in the bottom of my pocket.

"Don't worry about it, Jack," Grandpa said. "This one is on the house. In honor of your sudden hair loss." He smiled. "And go grab yourselves some RC Colas and peanuts to take with you too."

"Thank you, Mr. Chase," Piran said, grinning.

"Thanks, Grandpa," I said as we waved goodbye, the bells jingling behind us.

"You're so lucky your grandpa owns the Bait 'n Beer." Piran poured his peanuts into his cola. "So, with the mines closed and you not wantin' to be a miner anyhow, you think you might run his store someday?"

"Naw," I replied. "I want to be a forest ranger."

Piran spit soda out his nose. "A forest ranger?" He laughed. "Gotta have a forest first."

"I'm gonna bring it back," I said. "You just watch me."

We sat on the front stoop of the bait shop as we finished our drinks and watched the men striking in front of the Company on the far side of the river. The protest wasn't anywhere near as intense as it had been when the strike first began. Some of the men still paced back and forth, but most of 'em sat in lawn chairs raising their signs for passing cars. I recognized Dad's familiar silhouette standin' among them.

"Why don't they give it up?" Piran asked. "My dad says the Company will never hire back Union workers."

"They just want their old lives back." I frowned. "I wish my dad would find a job aboveground, something safe like your dad's job. Then he wouldn't have to worry about losing it either."

"If people keep leavin'," Piran replied, "there won't need to be a post office."

I sighed. It made me feel weird to see Dad and the other men put everything they had into what even I could see was a useless battle.

Piran and I put our glass bottles in the metal recyclin' crate and continued upstream next to Old Brawling Town Creek. The farther we walked, the greener things got. My mood lightened considerably—in fact, I couldn't stop smiling. It was happening. The longer the mine stayed closed, the better chance nature had, and it was moving in fast.

We hiked to our favorite fishing hole and waded to the big rock midstream, where we dropped our lines. Before long, we'd caught five hornyheads, but we threw them all back. Even upstream from the Company, it wasn't a good idea to eat fish from the river.

The sun beat down on us and I grew sleepy. I lay back on the rock, careful not to burn myself on the buckles of my overalls. That was pretty much my summer uniform, overalls and not much else. The buckles cooled underneath me and I let my muscles relax, feeling the heat from the rock soak into my bare skin. I heard a splash as Piran threw another hornyhead back into the water, but there was another sound too—a soft clicking.

"What is that noise?" Piran asked. "You hear it?" His head swung the other way. "There it is again."

"Bugs, I suppose," I replied.

"We never had bugs before," Piran said. "Why now?"

"They like the kudzu," I said. "Haven't you noticed things growing in?"

"I don't like it," he replied. "It don't look right."

"Better get used to it." I smiled. "Things are changin' in Coppertown."

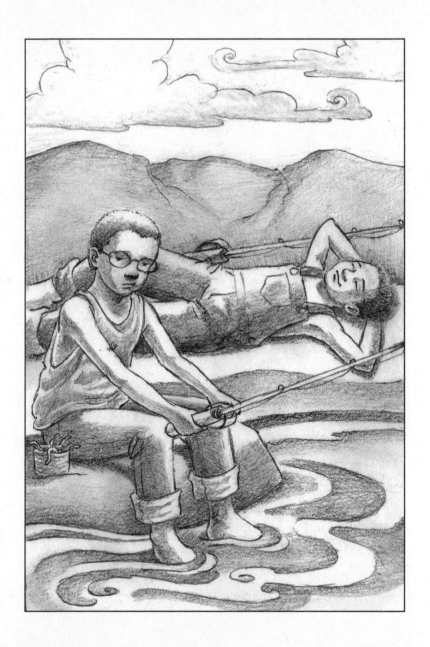

A cloud covered me in shadow just as we heard a voice from the shore.

"You boys better head home, yessirree. It's gonna rain, gonna rain," Crazy Coote called. He pointed at the sky. "It'll burnnn ya."

"Don't listen to him," Piran said. "He's nuts."

I felt bad for Coote, I did, but the way he looked at me like he could read my thoughts made me nervous. We made sure he was way out of sight before we left the rock and headed back to shore.

Coote was right about the rain, though. My arm ached as the storm clouds moved in. By the time Piran and I parted, it was coming down in heavy, ploppy drops that soaked me through. At least the rain didn't sting as bad as it used to. I ran up onto our front porch and tried to shake it off. But a shiver ran down my spine as I heard my parents inside arguing, again. I crept through the house creating a large puddle on the floor as I eavesdropped from the hallway.

"There aren't any jobs in town," Dad said. "I've been looking."

"Me too, but looking doesn't buy groceries, Ray," Mom replied. "You plan on picketing forever?"

"We've got my stipend from the Union," Dad argued, "and they're still workin' on it."

"It's not nearly enough! Besides, you don't honestly believe the Company is going to hire anybody back, do you?" she asked. "Give up on the mine, Ray. It already gave up on you."

"Have patience with me, Grace," Dad said. "All I've ever known is mining."

"We're barely getting by! I can't get the groceries we need, and Jack's outgrown most of his clothes." She raised her voice. "We can't live like this! You need steady work, a real paycheck, even if that means we have to move."

"Move? What are you talking about?" Dad asked. "This town is our home!"

"You think I want to leave?" Mom replied. "I don't want to go either. But, Ray, we have to be realistic."

My stomach lurched. *Move? No!*

I quietly made my way to the bathroom and shed my wet, heavy clothes. I dried off with a towel and rubbed it over my stubbly head. *Ouch!* I looked in the mirror. My new haircut had exposed my scalp, which was now bright red with sunburn. *Great, I'm gonna have to wear a hat from now on*, I fumed. *I will not let her buzz my head next year. I won't.*

In my bedroom I put on a long-sleeved T-shirt, a dry pair of overalls, and thick socks.

I lay on my bed and pulled the faded quilt Mom made over me. I couldn't get rid of the chill.

In the gray light of the rainy day, my blue walls appeared washed out and dirty. The locomotive border that ran around the top was peeling in the corners. My baseball trophies and the General Lee were dusty, and my desk, which used to belong to Grandpa, was chipped around the edges. *When did it all get so worn down?*

Again, my eyes were drawn to my poster of trees, a scene so different from Coppertown.

So it's not perfect, I thought. *But it's home, and I want to stay.*

I didn't realize I had dozed off until Mom gently shook me awake.

"Dinner's ready, Jack," she said. "White beans and cornbread."

"Mom, I don't want to move," I said.

"Well, I'm not gonna bring it to you," she said.

"No, I mean I don't want to leave Coppertown."

"What are you talking about?" she asked. "Oh, did you overhear your dad and me?" She sat on the end of my bed.

I nodded. "Things are gettin' better around here," I said. "Nature is coming back, things are growing."

"Honey, your garden might be doing well, but the town is drying up. Your dad needs a job."

"He'll find something," I said. "He has to."

"Oh, Jack, you're too young for all these worries. Heck, I am too." She ran her hand over the quilt she'd made for me, stopping on the flannel print that had been my baby blanket. "And you're getting too skinny. Come eat."

CHAPTER 25

Fairy Cross

Piran and I met at the bridge the next day and decided to check on the tadpoles up at the tailings pond. On the way there, I told Piran what I'd overheard my parents saying the night before. "We might have to move if my dad can't find work."

"Heck, I figured you'd be leaving eventually too." He frowned. "I'm gonna be the last kid left in Coppertown."

I didn't know what to say and tried to change the subject. "Did you see the article in the paper?" I asked.

"What?"

"The Rockets are in the championships."

"You got any more bad news there, Jack?" Piran said. "'Cause I don't think I'm quite depressed enough yet."

"Sorry."

But our moods changed completely when we got to the tadpoles.

"They've got legs!" Piran shouted.

"Except for their tails, they're almost frogs." I smiled. I felt like a proud papa.

The water had dried up with the warm weather like I expected. All that was left of the feeder creeks was a shallow pond, but the tiny frogs didn't need water for much longer before they'd be able to hop away. There was still enough for them to kick around and get the feel of their new limbs. Even Piran couldn't stop starin' at 'em.

As I sat and watched the tadpoles, I ran my fingers through the sand on the bank. Sunlight glittered on a small object. "Piran, look at this." I dug it out. It was a rock, no bigger than a quarter, but it had two faceted rods that ran straight through each other forming a perfect cross.

"Oh cool!" Piran said. "That's a fairy cross!"

"Since when are you into rocks?"

"Ever since I wanted to be a miner is all." Piran rolled his eyes. "They're really called staurolite crystals, but most folks just call 'em fairy crosses. Outside of the Copper Basin I hear they're pretty rare, but we have more here than anywhere else. Hasn't your grandpa told you about 'em?"

"No." I shook my head and looked at my friend with new eyes. All the bad grades and laziness—I figured there wasn't anything Piran really cared about. But here it was. His face lit up like a firecracker as he told me about fairy crosses.

"Well, one story is that when the Cherokee were forced to leave this land, their tears fell to the ground and froze in the shape of little crosses. Did you know the Cherokee used to play sports where our ball field is? It was some old version of lacrosse. I found an arrowhead up there once.

"There's another story about the fairy crosses. Some say when Jesus was crucified, the fairies here in the Appalachians could feel it and cried. Their tears fell to the ground in the shape of crosses.

"They're considered really good luck. Even President Teddy Roosevelt carried one in his pocket."

"That's cool! You should have it." I grinned and handed it to him.

"Naw, I can't. You found it," he said.

"I have my frogs," I said. "And you have your rocks."

He held it up to the light and spun it around with a smile. "Thanks!"

Danged if he didn't find another one a short time

later and give it to me. We had good luck times two, and Lord knows we needed it.

CHAPTER 26
Blackberries

S ummer was in its prime. The little hairs on my arms stood out bleached blond against my brown skin, and the last signs of where my cast had been were officially gone. The soles of my feet were as tough as horse's hooves, and my baseball hat was permanently attached to my head.

On the first day of July, Mom popped in my room. "It's blackberry pickin' day, Jack. Why don't you call Piran and see if he wants to join us? We're going someplace new."

Picking blackberries meant driving outside of Coppertown! I leaped out of bed.

"Put on boots and a long-sleeved shirt," Mom called from down the hall.

"I don't need shoes," I hollered back.

"You will where we're going! Not an inch of skin showing, y'hear?"

My boots felt weird and too tight, like weights smotherin' my toes. Long sleeves made my arms feel like they were wrapped in plaster again. I wasn't used to having anything against my skin, and I didn't like it.

Mom had torn the kitchen apart. She was buried deep in the pantry, rattling metal and glass. "Jack, grab these, will ya?"

She handed me box after box of half-pint mason jars and a basket full of metal lids and rings. She dusted herself off as she climbed out. "I wanted to see how many I had." She smiled. "I'd say a good many!"

Every summer Mom would go to the Spencer farm to buy fresh fruits and veggies and then put up jars of tomatoes, fruit, jam, and beans—she loved to can. She said it was a carryover from her Beech Mountain days when they used to put up all sorts of food for winter.

"Nice thing about blackberries is they're free," she said. "Grab three buckets and the two coolers from your dad's metal shop while I make some sandwiches." She packed lunch into the smaller cooler and we loaded everything into the trunk of the car.

We were about to leave when Mom stopped and ran

back to the house. "Almost forgot!" She returned with a can of bug spray—the logo was faded it was so old. "We're gonna need this."

We drove down to pick up Piran, who was also dressed in boots and a long-sleeved shirt. Mom nodded her approval and called out to Mrs. Quinn, "I'll have him home before sunset, Doris." We waved and headed out with high spirits.

Mom turned on the radio and we all sang along to the new song by Dolly Parton, Emmylou Harris, and Linda Ronstadt about wildflowers not caring where they grow, because they're survivors. Mom's pretty voice fit right in with the trio.

We headed west into the Tohachee River Gorge, but cut north on that same winding road I'd seen Eli go up when we'd gone pumpkin huntin' before Halloween. The trees that had looked like Fruity Pebbles last fall were now covered in leaves of a million shades of green. The longer we drove, the more lush it became. Piran and I gaped out the windows at the Georgia pines that towered above us with their deep green needles and spiky gray trunks. Light fell across the road, playing tricks on our eyes as we sped through the mottled pattern of calm blue shadows and blinding sun.

"Where we goin'?" I asked.

"To a new blackberry patch your aunt Livvy told me about—up in a place called Devil's Den, or at least that's what it used to be called."

My ears perked up. *Why does that sound familiar?*

"How'd it get that name?" Piran asked.

"There used to be a lot of moonshiners in these parts," she said. "It was pretty wild in its day. But that's all gone now."

After an hour, she turned off the pavement into the woods and slowly drove up a long-forgotten dirt road. The car rocked wildly over the bumps and small ditches caused by rainwater runoff.

"There's an old log cabin development up here," Mom told us. "Remember a few years back when some developers from the city were gonna put in vacation rentals? They cut the road in and cleared some of the lots before they went bankrupt or somethin'. Now it's one gigantic blackberry patch."

About a quarter mile in, a small road cut off to the right to a run-down trailer. Animal skins were nailed to its sides and a hand-scrawled KEEP OUT! sign was nailed to a tree out front. But what really caught my attention was the yellow Jeep parked out front. "What's Eli Munroe doin' way out here?" I asked. A puzzle was coming together in my head, but it was like rememberin' Grandma Chase— the pieces were fuzzy and I couldn't make sense of 'em.

"I... I don't know," Mom said and revved the engine to speed by.

The weeds closed in around us as we drove another twenty minutes or so. They brushed against the car and slapped our arms until we rolled up the windows to keep from getting cut, or worse, losing an eye.

Finally, the dark woods gave way to a large open area, silvery white. We stopped right in the middle.

When Mom turned the key, a loud buzzing noise—as loud as a sawmill—replaced the sound of the engine.

"What is that?!" Piran yelled over the din. He covered his ears.

"Cicadas," Mom shouted back. "It was on the news the other night. It's their thirteen-year swarm. They're really thick this year."

"Chickadees?" Piran asked.

"No, cicadas," she replied. "Sih-kay-duhs."

Piran couldn't say it right for nothin'. "I've never heard anything like it!" he said. "Do they bite or sting?"

"Cicadas won't bother you, but the mosquitoes and chiggers will. C'mere, boys, let me spray you." She covered us with so much bug spray from our necks down that we were wet with the stuff. Then she told us to close our eyes tight as she sprayed our heads. I was a toxic cloud.

Piran looked at me with a frown and whispered, "I better not be getting no bug bites."

Mom sprayed herself too. "Yu'uns grab a bucket and get picking!"

I walked up to the tangled vines that created a dense wall of thorns in front of me. It took a minute for my eyes to get used to lookin' for berries, but once they adjusted, berries were all I could see. There were still some red ones, but mostly I saw the deep purple masses of ripe, bumpy blackberries.

I had to try the first one—it wouldn't have been right not to. It was so ripe, it fell into my hand when I touched it. I pressed it to the roof of my mouth with my tongue.

The warm juice squirted, bitter and sweet at the same time, while the berry skin melted.

Piran pelted me with a handful of blackberries and I threw some back. It was an all-out blackberry war until Mom said, "Wastin' blackberries just means less pie!"

Piran and I froze. My mom made the best blackberry pie in Coppertown. We hunkered down and got to work.

The next one I picked I dropped into my bucket with a satisfying *plunk*. I grabbed handfuls at a time and dropped them in until the sound went from *plunk* to *thump*, from the berries landin' on top of each other.

It was an awkward job. I kept getting snagged on the thorns and spent more time trying to get loose than picking berries.

Piran hollered, "They keep falling down!"

"You have to cup your hand under them, sugar," Mom said and came over to give us a proper lesson in blackberry pickin'. She looked at the scratches on my hands. "If you move really slow, the thorns won't grab you. Here, watch me."

She gracefully stretched her arm deep into a thicket and cupped her hand under a cluster of berries. Her fingers tickled them loose until they fell gently into her

palm. She removed her arm just as slowly and didn't get snagged once.

"See?" She smiled.

"Shouldn't we be worried 'bout bears or mountain lions out here?" Piran asked.

"I imagine the sound of the car scared 'em off," she said. "But I like to sing while I pick so I don't accidentally surprise anything."

We went back to our patches and she started singing "Keep on the Sunny Side." Piran and I joined in at the chorus. Then we sang "Carry Me Across the Mountain" and "Angel Band"—old tunes we all knew from Music Fridays.

Picking berries like Mom showed us worked much better. I filled my bucket several times over and dumped the berries into the cooler. Between the singin', the warm sun, the cicadas buzzing, and the slow moving, I was calm right down to my toes.

Which I suppose is why I didn't notice the snake until he tried to squirm out from under my foot. I looked down, glad I'd only stepped on him lightly—and smiled at his pretty copper colors and the interesting pattern that ran all over his back. We didn't have snakes in Coppertown, so I had no idea what kind he was. He had a sharply angled head and was sort of fat. *It's no wonder he's stuck*, I thought. I lifted up my foot and he scooted away, more confused than scared.

"Cool snake," I said.

"Snake?" Piran yelled from ten feet away.

"What?!" Mom shouted from twenty.

"I was standing on a snake," I hollered.

"What did it look like?" Mom asked.

When I described it to her, I thought she was gonna have a heart attack. "Law' me, that was a copperhead!" she said. "Come out of there right now!"

We rushed to the car and stopped to catch our breath. "How many buckets did you fill?" she asked but didn't wait for me to answer. "We probably have enough for today."

We stared at our haul in the cooler, which was full to the brim. "This'll make some good pies, and we've got enough for canning too," Mom said. "Let's go find a nice spot for lunch."

We piled into the car and drove back down the bumpy road. I noticed Eli's Jeep was gone and wondered what was in that trailer that would make him drive all the way out here. I doubted Eli was pickin' blackberries.

When we got to the main road, we hung a right and rolled down the windows, letting in a gust of hot air, but also lettin' our bug-spray-and-sweat smell *out*. After a few miles we were back to the Tohachee River. We parked at a pull-off, where the river ran shallow and white as the water tumbled over rocks.

We grabbed the lunch cooler and sat on a huge flat boulder that jutted out into the river. I stared at the tulip poplars and pines that reached out over the banks as we ate peanut butter sandwiches and drank RC Colas.

"It's hard to believe Coppertown used to look like this," I said.

"I suppose," Piran said, "but I like the way it is now."

"The Red Hills do have their beautiful moments," Mom said. "We can see as far as the horizon with nothing to block our view."

I looked across the river to the bank on the other side. She was right about that. I couldn't see more than a hundred feet from the forest being so thick, full of ferns and bushes covered with flaming orange flowers. But I liked *that* better.

As I stared, the biggest bird I ever saw swooped down

right in front of us with two smaller birds flying tight on its tail, squawkin' up a storm.

"Whoa!" Piran said. "Was that a hawk?"

"I think so," Mom said. "The smaller birds must have been chasing him out of their territory." It was so graceful and strong—I couldn't believe something that big could fly through the trees without crashing into them.

Everything around me was moving. Leaves swayed in the breeze, scattering light between them. Birds and squirrels jumped from branch to branch, bugs and butterflies zigged and zagged, busy with their work, and the river gurgled and changed colors in the sun. Coppertown was so incredibly quiet and still in comparison. I was overwhelmed by so much life surroundin' me.

"Wish I had my fishin' pole," Piran said and pointed to a huge trout as it slipped through an eddy. "I bet we could eat the fish here."

Across the road I saw a trail cutting into the woods. "Hey, Mom, mind if Piran and I explore some before we go?"

"Okay," she said and lay back on the rock. "I wouldn't mind soaking up some sunshine. But don't be too long, and yu'uns be careful, y'hear?"

I smiled. "Yes, ma'am." It was nice to see Mom relax for a change.

Piran and I pushed branches out of our way and hiked up the trail about a quarter mile.

"What is that?" he asked and pointed to a light brown shell of a bug clinging to a tree. It had two front legs like pinchers, and a split down the back. I gently pulled it from the bark. It was so fragile. I cupped my hands around it to keep from crushin' it.

"Oh, that is gross," Piran said.

"No it's not. It's neat!" I replied.

I collected three more shells as we walked. The air was cool and smelled spicy with blooms. Layers of leaves and pine needles crunched softly beneath our feet. We were surrounded by sounds. I couldn't stop smiling—a forest was an amazing thing.

We followed the trail as it sank down into a shallow little valley and came to a small clearing with an old stone chimney covered in vines.

Piran stepped down and *crack!* "What the..." He pushed some leaves out of the way. "It's a mason jar."

The closer we looked the more we saw. There were dozens of them scattered all around the chimney.

"Y'know what this is?" I said. "This here is the site of an old moonshine still. I remember Grandpa Chase telling me about 'em."

"You think?" Piran asked.

We looked around at all the man-made signs of times past. There was a barrel, a bucket, and some pipe, but it was all rusted or broken.

"I bet the still sat right here," I said.

I imagined I could smell the sour mash and hear the gunshots as the revenuers chased the bootleggers away. I found a mason jar that was in perfect shape except for being a little dirty. I put the bug shells inside and brought it back to Mom.

"It probably was an old moonshine site," she agreed. "Like I said, there used to be a lot of that around here." She held the jar up to the sun. "These are cicada shells. See where they crawled out?"

"Is that why there's a split down their backs?" I asked.

"Yup. This is an exoskeleton."

"Gross." Piran shivered.

Mom just smiled. "Yu'uns ready to go?"

I wasn't. I could have stayed there forever.

At home, I helped wash the berries through a strainer and put them in bags for the refrigerator. The sink was filled with purple juice. I popped a few more berries into my mouth but Mom swatted my hand.

"Don't eat them, Jack!" she said. "I'm gonna can whatever I don't use for the pies."

Sure enough, when I went in the kitchen for lunch the next day, I found it covered in purple juice, glass jars, and tall cooking pots full of jam and boiling water.

"You want to help?" Mom asked with a grin.

"It's burning up in here!" I said. She had all the doors open and fans stationed at the front and back tryin' to cool things off, but it didn't make much difference. "No thanks."

Sweat dripped down my face as I ate my sandwich as fast as I could.

I watched Mom use tongs to lift jars of hot jam from the pot of boiling water. She lined them up on the counter where they twinkled like purple jewels.

Pop! Pop!

"Pops o' joy." She smiled.

"Why do they make that sound?" I asked.

"When I boil the jars and then cool them, I'm creating a vacuum," she replied. "The pop means they're sealed."

"Can I try some?"

"Oh, they're too hot right now, but I'll put a jar in the fridge for later," she said.

The newspaper lay on the corner of the kitchen table. I couldn't help but notice the mug shots that took up most of the front page. "Two Men Arrested for Growing Marijuana Near Hell's Holler," the headline read.

Marijuana. Although neither mug shot was of Eli Munroe, it all suddenly came together in my mind. *That's what Eli's been up to. It explains everything...*

"Mom, did you see this?" I asked. "Isn't Hell's Holler right near where we were in Devil's Den—like a ridge away?"

She put a kitchen towel on top of the paper to cover the headline. "Yes," she said in a fluster. "We'll just go back to my old blackberry patch next year."

"I guess Devil's Den hasn't changed much after all," I said. No more moonshine—nowadays it was pot.

CHAPTER 27

Independence Day

Saturday was the Fourth of July. Nobody could celebrate our nation's birthday better than Coppertown, Tennessee.

We went to the church first thing in the mornin' for homemade buckwheat pancakes and hot cane syrup. Piran and I went back four times each. Everybody seemed to be in a good mood for a change. Happy conversation bounced off the cement block walls of the community room. There was so much red, white, and blue everywhere, I grew dizzy with the colors.

Mom made Dad promise not to talk about the strike for the day, so he didn't say much of anything. Meanwhile, she chatted with friends and slipped me some change for the fair. "Don't spend it all in one place," she said sarcastically and laughed. I knew it was more than we could afford, so I smiled and thanked her. She squeezed my hand.

My stomach felt like a water balloon about to pop as we left the church and headed for the ball field. I threw my shoes into the back seat of our car on the way. Mom could make me wear a shirt, but there was no way I was gonna wear shoes all day.

As Piran and I walked over, I told him about the newspaper story and my theory about Eli. "It's the only thing that makes sense. Why else would his Jeep have been up there? And do you remember all those light bulbs that fell out of his car last winter? He was growin' seedlings—just like I was doing, only his were illegal. I bet he was growing 'em in that trailer."

"God, Jack! What are we gonna do about it?"

"I don't know. But remember what I heard Sheriff Elder sayin' about the pot fields? One was in Hell's Holler and the other was in Devil's Den. It's only a matter of time before they bust Eli too. His field has to be right near where we were pickin' blackberries."

"This sucks. I wonder if Hannah knows..."

We were silent the rest of the way over—each of us deep in thought. But the excitement of the day couldn't keep us quiet for long.

They were still setting up tables and tents at the ball field when we got there, but the air buzzed with promise. Mom had already dropped off her blackberry pie for the baking competition. Piran and I watched as they turned the city's flatbed wrecker truck into a stage for gospel and bluegrass. The hamburger stand fired up their grill, and despite my full belly, I couldn't wait for lunch as I breathed in the mouthwatering smell.

The Boy Scouts set up a demonstration campsite. Piran and I walked quickly by to avoid the director, Mr. Brown. Two years before, Buster got in a fight with his son. We'd all gotten in trouble for cheerin' it on, and Mr. Brown still held a grudge.

With tinny chugs, antique cars lined up along the outfield fence. We walked the entire length, checking under the hoods like we knew what we were looking at. I oohed over a candy-red '57 Corvette with a white leather interior. Piran tried to grab the wheel, but the owner barked, "Don't touch!"

So we headed for our favorite thing—the dunkin' machine.

"Who do you think we'll get to dunk this year?" Piran asked.

"It was Principal Slaughter last year," I said. "How

they gonna top that?"

"No way!" Piran said. "Sheriff Elder is getting in! Let's go!"

"Piran, you can't sink the sheriff!"

"You watch me!"

I swear Piran reminded me of Buster sometimes—he just didn't think things through. With Eli's future in jeopardy, now was not the time to be attracting the sheriff's attention, maybe puttin' pieces together in his head: Piran led to Hannah, who led to Eli, who led to pot. It was all too close for comfort and put Hannah in danger besides. Piran may not have liked it, and I didn't either, but Eli was still his brother-in-law—family.

Despite my protest, Piran bought three tries for a quarter each and got into his pitcher's stance.

"Is that Piran Quinn there?" the sheriff asked as he perched atop the little ledge, his toes barely touching the water below. "You think you can take me down, son?"

"I'm gonna try!" Piran wound up and threw as hard as he could at the round red target on the side of the bin. The ball whizzed by without touching it.

Sheriff Elder guffawed. "I think I'll be stayin' dry through this one!"

Piran's ears turned red and he wound up again. This

time he nicked the edge, but not hard enough to trigger the lever.

"Yup, dry as a bone," Sheriff Elder said and smiled menacingly.

"Don't do it," I whispered, trying one last time.

Piran looked at me with a glint in his eye and nodded. "Don't worry, I got it now."

He spit, straightened up, and wound the ball. It flew from his hand like a bullet, straight at the target.

Kasploosh! Down went Sheriff Elder.

"Good arm, Quinn." The sheriff coughed as he came up and looked at Piran with a smile that wasn't altogether friendly. I could almost see the wheels turning in his head. *That's the boy whose sister married that troublemaker, Eli...*

"C'mon, let's get out of here." I tugged at Piran, who walked away struttin' like a turkey. "I don't think that was a good idea," I said.

"Ah, that was great!" Piran crowed.

The music was firing up, so we ran to the stage. Piran's dad was up there playing clawhammer banjo with his group, Dreadful Noise. They played "Wayfaring Stranger," and then "Cluck Ole Hen." I couldn't keep still when they got to "Arkansas Traveler." I tried to buck dance with the crowd growing in front of the stage, but my two left feet wouldn't let me do more than stomp around and kick up dust. Piran danced until the dust got to be too much.

"I gotta sit," he gasped and pulled out his inhaler.

"I'll get us some colas," I hollered over the music.

We watched the print skirts and overalls whirl by as the band played "Cold Frosty Morn." Through the crowd, we caught a glimpse of…

"Oh man," Piran groaned.

Speak o' the devil.

Eli was walking with Hannah. She was barely showing—you'd only notice if you knew she was pregnant, but of course everybody did. She and Eli ignored the stares and whispers and walked at the edge of the crowd. I couldn't take my eyes off them. From a distance, it looked like they were arguin'. *Maybe she does know about the pot.*

"How are they doing?" I asked.

"She doesn't talk to us much," Piran said, "but I heard through the grapevine that he's gone a lot."

We looked at each other and I was sure we were thinking the same thing: *He's been at his pot field.* Something in me tugged.

Toward midday we figured we could probably pack

some more food into our bellies. The burger stand smelled so good, I could've chewed on the air. We both bought cheeseburgers and loaded them with ketchup, mayonnaise, lettuce, tomatoes, onions, and Mrs. Spencer's pickle relish. Our burgers were twice as tall by the time we left the fixings table and made our way back through the crowd. The ketchup squished out the sides of my burger and ran down my hands, but I didn't care.

"I bet I could eat this whole thing in three bites," Piran said.

"I bet I could too, but I'm not gonna," I replied. I only had enough money for one burger and planned on making it last as long as possible. I took tiny, little bites to prove it.

When I got home, I actually took a nap. I felt like a baby doing it, but being so full knocked me right out. I awoke several hours later with my stomach growling. Okay, maybe it was more upset than hungry, but I wasn't done yet.

Dad squirted lighter fluid on the coals, creating a four-foot-high flame on the grill in the backyard. I helped Mom set up a card table and placed a rock on the pile of napkins threatenin' to scatter in the light breeze. Everybody on the south side of the river gathered in our backyard since we had the best view of Tater Hill, and they all brought food. We had to set up three card tables to hold everything.

Macaroni and cheese seemed to be the most popular dish to bring this year—yum! I was enjoying being full for a change and went back for a second helping. To top it off, I had a slice of Mom's blackberry pie, which had won first place at the fair, of course.

"It's my secret ingredient." Mom smiled. Even Dad didn't know what it was.

She'd made three pies—one for the church raffle, one for the judging, and one for us, so there was plenty for us to judge for ourselves.

She deserved the prize all right.

Little kids ran around with sparklers while everybody set up their folding chairs facin' town. The men made bets on whether the volunteer fire department would catch everything on fire again this year. Grandpa Chase played a few reels on his fiddle while we all waited for it to grow dark.

About that time, Eli and Hannah made an appearance. They put out two folding chairs next to Mr. and Mrs. Quinn—obviously at Hannah's insistence. Nobody looked too comfortable about it.

I kept staring at 'em—watching Hannah. Even with her married to another man, I couldn't help how I felt. I wanted to protect her. So when Eli went for seconds, I went back for thirds.

I waited until Mr. Dilbeck got a hot dog and left— and we were alone. "Hey, Eli," I said as I pretended to peruse the food.

"Huh? Oh, hey...Jack, right?" Like he didn't know who I was.

"Yeah. Hey, you see that article in today's paper about the marijuana bust over in Hell's Holler?"

"Yeah, so?"

"Well, I overheard Sheriff Elder talking last month. They've been monitoring a growin' field over in Devil's Den too. He said they had cameras set up and were just waitin' for enough evidence to bust whoever is growin' there. Whoever it is, next time they show up, they're probably gonna get arrested."

Eli stopped putting food on his plate and coughed. "Why you tellin' me this, Jack?"

"Because Hannah's pregnant. And she needs a husband who's around to take care of her."

We stood there in frozen, awkward silence for a moment, until I couldn't stand it anymore. "Anyhow,

I'll be seein' ya." Even though he was smart as a bag of hammers, I hoped Eli got the message.

I went over and grabbed a folding chair next to Piran.

"Hi, Jack," Hannah said as I sat down. I guess what they say about pregnant women is true—she glowed like a light shone from right inside her, and I knew I'd done the right thing.

Long before the actual show started, the battle of the bottle rockets began. Coppertown straddled the state line, so roadside fireworks stands were plentiful. Even in tough times, people splurged to celebrate America's birthday. Since the town sat in a bowl, people could shoot fireworks back and forth from the houses on the slopes until the sky was lit up from every direction. It was like watchin' a tennis match with explosives.

"That must be the Dilbecks' house," somebody said. "They always buy the big ones."

"That must be the Pritchards' over there," somebody else said and laughed. "Those are some piss-poor fireworks!"

Finally the main show began. Booms echoed off

the storefronts in town and throughout the valley. We oohed and aahed and named each one our new favorite. Occasionally the wind blew our direction carrying the burnt smell of gunpowder—it didn't smell nearly as bad as the clouds from the Company, though, so it didn't bother us. The smoke created light gray patches against the dark blue sky. For the grand finale, the VFD launched blooms of green, red, and blue along with a rocket that shot up with a high-pitched whistle and showered the sky with long white sparkly tails.

I couldn't help but watch how they reflected in Hannah's eyes.

Everybody declared it the best show ever, although it was much smaller and shorter than in previous years. Piran and I agreed the year the VFD accidentally lit the entire box of fireworks at one time was still the winner. It was amazing that nobody had gotten hurt.

The crowd slowly broke up as people grabbed blankets and chairs and meandered home.

My shoulders were still warm, my middle was round as a barrel, my conscience was clear, and my eyelids were too heavy to keep open. I rolled into bed with a grin that wouldn't wipe off and fell asleep as soon as my head hit the pillow.

CHAPTER 28
Bird!

When Piran and I headed to Old Brawling Town Creek to fish later that week, it was hot as fire—the kind of heat that zapped all the energy right out of you. The fish must have felt it too, because they went deep and we didn't catch a one.

We sat staring at our slack fishing lines, our feet hangin' in the water.

"Think your grandpa would let us borrow some tubes from the bait shop?" Piran asked. "We could go tubing down the river."

"Maybe." I yawned but didn't move.

"Ow!" Piran yelped and slapped his arm. "Somethin' bit me!"

"Probably a mosquito," I said.

"Chick-a-dees and now mosquitoes," Piran complained. "We never had bugs before."

"I told you things are changing. First come plants, then come bugs, and then come the critters who eat the bugs—like frogs." I smiled.

Piran scratched his bite. "Well, I don't like it," he huffed. "It's too hot out here. Let's go see if we can get some movie money out of my dad. At least the theater would be cool."

On the way into town, I was thinking about what other sort of critters, along with the frogs, would be moving in to eat the new bugs, when we passed Crazy Coote again.

"Gonna break the strike, yessirree," he said, looking at me. "That's a what they're gonna do."

We walked wide around him, Piran scratchin' his bug bite the whole time.

"Stop it," I complained.

"Why? It makes it feel better," Piran said.

"I don't know, but my mom never let me scratch when my arm was broken."

Downtown, everything glared white in the hot sun.

People ran quickly into the few businesses that were still open to get to the air-conditioning. Dilbeck's Pharmacy was packed. Even grown-ups walked out with ice-cream cones.

We stared in the window at the long counter with its chrome and red vinyl seats.

Piran said, "Maybe I should ask my dad for ice cream money instead."

Suddenly I saw a fluttering motion reflected in the glass.

I turned around to see a small brown-and-white-striped bird land on the lamppost across the street.

I was so surprised, I pointed and yelled, "A bird!"

"On Water Street?" Mrs. McCay stopped and looked. "Of all places, law' me."

The town came to a standstill as everybody stared. Word spread fast and people even came out of their businesses to see. As we watched, the tiny bird chirped the prettiest little song. It sounded kind of like, "Sweet, sweet, sweet, as ever it may be."

Mrs. McCay smiled. "It's a sparrow."

"Really?" I asked. It was like the picture I drew for Mom at Christmas, but without the purple.

"I'd think somethin' with such a nice name would be prettier than that," Piran said.

"It's the prettiest thing I've ever seen," Mrs. McCay replied.

I looked closer at the bird's round lines and delicate fan of feathers as it opened its wings to fly away.

"Me too," I decided. *It's the prettiest thing ever—just the way it is.*

Mr. Quinn was deep in conversation when we entered the post office.

"They're building a new carpet mill in Dalton," Mr. Thomas said. "They need electricians, carpenters, machinists, the whole lot."

"Just fifty miles south of here?" Mr. Quinn replied. "That's good news for the miners."

"Well, it won't pay as good," Mr. Harmon said. "Heck, nothing could replace mining pay back in the good old days."

"Even so," Mr. Quinn said. "The men need jobs."

I couldn't believe my ears—I had to tell Dad! I charged out the door, making the bell clang and clatter behind me.

I ran as fast as I could through town to the picket line. The closer I got, the more I could hear somethin' was going on.

CHAPTER 29

Scabs

The miners were in an uproar when I got to the Company. Everybody was on their feet, shouting and stabbing their signs into the air. I searched for my dad in the crowd.

Mr. Hill shouted through his bullhorn, "They've sold the entire plant to a business in South America." He read an announcement from the Company lawyers. "And they've hired temporary workers to break it down!"

As a busload of ragged-looking men worked its way through, the crowd went wild. The miners cursed and shouted, "SCABS! SCABS! SCABS!"

I'd never seen so many people so angry. It made me nervous.

Just when I thought it couldn't get any worse,

I noticed Eli Munroe sittin' toward the back of the bus, trying to crouch down out of view.

I wasn't the only one who spotted him.

"Traitor!" somebody yelled and threw a rock at the bus. It ricocheted off and hit me square on the forehead. I flinched at the sharp pain. I looked down at my hand. Blood covered my fingers. Somebody grabbed my arm and pulled me away from the mob.

"Jack, you shouldn't be here!" Mr. Barnes said. "Dammit, who's throwing rocks?" He pulled a bandanna from his pocket and mopped at my forehead. "It's bleeding pretty bad. Hold this against it."

"I'm lookin' for my dad," I gasped.

"His shift ended over an hour ago," Mr. Barnes said.

"He's at home?" I tried to hand back the bandanna.

"You keep that pressed to your head until your mama can clean you up," he said. "And Jack, tell your dad the Company's closing and they've brought in scabs to break it down. They're doin' us so wrong."

I ran back through town, across the bridge, and up the hill holding the bandanna to my head as best I could. Even so,

I was hot and out of breath with blood runnin' down my face by the time I reached home. A few drops strayed into the corner of my mouth, tasting of metal.

Knowing better than to look for Dad in the house, I ran straight to his metal shop. I could hear him tinkering inside.

"Jack! What happened?" he shouted when I yanked the door open.

"I got hit by a rock down at the picket line," I said. "The Company's shuttin' down and brought in scabs to take it apart. Mr. Barnes told me to tell you."

"DAMN!" He slammed down his pliers. "Well, that's it then." Dad sighed heavily and put his hands on his hips. It was like something in him had snapped. He rubbed his face, and when his hands came away, his eyes were clearer than I'd seen them in months.

"C'mon and let's get you cleaned up," he said. We rushed to the bathroom in the house. "I'm glad your mother's out. She'd have a fit if she saw you like this," he said. "I don't think you need stitches, though. Looks like it just grazed ya."

He washed my cut and swabbed it with iodine. It burned like fire and I cringed at the sting.

"Stay still. It's not that bad."

Why did grown-ups always say "it's not that bad" when something was as bad as it could possibly be?

As he pulled out a bandage from the first aid kit, I asked, "So what's a scab?"

"You mean like you're gonna have on your head?"

"No, like what they were calling those guys down at the strike," I said.

"A scab is somebody who crosses a picket line to work," he growled. "Somebody who's got no soul."

"If they don't have a soul," I replied, "they got nothin' to fly through the spirit hole at church when they die."

"I suppose not."

"They were awfully sad looking," I said.

"I'm sure they were desperate men, Jack. Even worse off than us," he replied.

"Eli Munroe was with them."

"Really?" Dad shook his head in disgust. "He finally got the job he always wanted, workin' at the Company. Course, he just made enemies out of the entire town."

I didn't know what to think about Eli. He must've given up on the pot field, or he wouldn't have been there. But his backup plan was a bad one too.

"I honestly thought the Company would try to work

it out with us." Dad took a deep breath. "I guess it was just wishful thinkin.'"

"Dad, Mr. Quinn was talking to Mr. Harmon at the post office," I said. "There's jobs at a new carpet mill in Dalton."

Dad stuck a large bandage onto my head. "You are just full of news today," he said as he crinkled the bandage wrapper in his hand. He threw it in the trash can. "Come on."

"We goin' to the picket line?" I asked.

"No, son," he said heavily. "We're going to the post office."

On the way there, I told him about the sparrow.

"Jack, there hasn't been a bird around these parts in decades," he said.

"It's here because the Company hasn't been running," I replied. "There aren't enough fumes to kill 'em anymore."

"You've been listenin' to your grandpa again," he said and rubbed the back of his neck. "But I guess... I think you might be right."

I never saw my dad look at me the way he did right then—it made me stand a little taller.

At sunrise, Mom and I waved goodbye to Dad and some of the other miners as they drove away.

Dad had called the others right after he got the details about the carpet mill. "Maybe they'll have enough work for all of us," he'd said.

Mom and I looked down the road long after the dust cloud settled.

"When they gonna be back?" I asked.

"I guess when they have jobs." She sighed.

"I put a fairy cross in Dad's pocket."

"Yeah? Where'd you learn about those?" Mom smiled and rubbed my head. "Want me to help you weed your garden, Jack? I can't believe how it's growing. You must have a green thumb or something. You're like Johnny Appleseed—even your dogwood is doing okay."

It was Friday, music night, so Mom and I grabbed our folding chairs and walked down to the river park. The music was great, as always, but the air was thick with tension. It was like the entire town was holdin' its breath waiting for the men to come home—good news was almost too scary to wish for. Everybody seemed determined to have a good time and laughed a little too hard, but it just wasn't working. Mom didn't join in at all.

"Grace, come sing," Grandpa called to her.

"Another night, Pa," she said and continued to watch the river rush by.

The phone was ringing when we got back to the house. Mom ran to pick it up.

She smiled at me and nodded—Dad. But as he talked, her smile faded. "Where are you gonna stay? Oh, okay," she said. "It was fine. Same ol' thing. We miss you."

I raised my eyebrows when she hung up the phone.

"The man who's hiring wasn't there today, and your dad and the miners aren't the only ones who showed up for jobs." She sighed. "They're gonna stick around until they can talk to the supervisor. It might not be 'til Monday."

"Where are they gonna sleep?" I asked.

"Hm?" She looked worried. "Oh, in the car."

Desperate times deserve desperate measures, Aunt Livvy had said.

CHAPTER 30

Frogs

With mixed feelings, I watched the Company hum back to life. The railway started runnin' again and trucks came and went nonstop, but the miners had nothing to do with it. Nobody knew anything about the replacement workers—they didn't venture into town, not even Eli. He probably would've gotten beat up if he did.

Everybody was complaining at church on Sunday morning. They figured if the Company was willing to hire Eli Munroe, it didn't say much about the intelligence level of the rest of the scabs. The general opinion was that the replacement workers had no idea what they were doin'.

"It's dangerous," Grandpa said when he stopped by after church. "Just wait and see how long before somebody spills something or goes and gets himself blowed up. It's bound to happen."

Mom just mumbled, "Hmm."

"I heard they were dumpin' leftover sludge straight into the river yesterday," he said. "Can you believe that? They're supposed to dump up at the tailings ponds."

I bolted upright. "The tailings ponds? You think they're using Old Number Two?" *My frogs!*

"They're supposed to." He shook his head. "Too lazy, I imagine. They've got no respect at all."

"Mom, I gotta go." I jumped up, ran out the door, and didn't stop.

"What? Jack, be home for supper!" she yelled behind me.

I ran as fast as I could to the tailings pond, not slowin' down once. I was panting and out of breath when I finally got there.

New tire tracks were pressed into the dirt road leading to the gate, which now stood wide open. My heart dropped to my feet and I stopped, afraid of what I might find.

Please, I thought. *Please let them be okay.*

I tried to swallow as I walked around to the water that held my frogs, but my throat was dry as a bone.

As I got close, I knew something was different. The air had that putrid smell again and the weeds and grasses, which had been doing so well, were brown and wilting. I rushed to the pond.

No!

Little frogs floated on the surface of the water, their white bellies upturned. A few more developed frogs lay on the bank, their paper-thin skin drawn tightly over their tiny frames. My legs suddenly felt like rubber and I sank to the ground. I wrapped my arms around my knees and let the tears flow down my cheeks. I was too late. Every last one of them was dead.

I cried hard like I hadn't done since I was a kid, but I didn't care. It wasn't right.

Stupid Company, I thought. I looked across the tailings pond. *It isn't natural. It's not supposed to look like this.* The Company had scarred so much of my home. Our town, set down in its valley, wasn't all that different from the little frog pond.

If they killed my frogs so easily, what are they doing to us?

I thought about Uncle Amon and Mrs. Ledford and all the other funerals I'd been to in my life. *Is it normal for someone my age to have been to so many?*

Through my sobs, I slowly became aware of a faint

chirping noise. I looked over my shoulder, following the sound. There, about three feet away from the pond, was one little frog. I dried my eyes and crawled toward him. He just looked at me, blinked, and let me gently scoop him into my hands.

"Do you have any more friends, little man?" I asked. He chirped as if replying, *No*.

I cupped my other hand over the top of him, creating a safe cave, and looked around, but he was the only one still alive.

I walked home slowly, careful not to close my hands too tightly. I thought about all of the little frog's lost brothers and felt like smoke was comin' out of my ears.

"It's all their fault," I said out loud and kicked a soda can with a tinny *ka-tink*. "I'm glad the Company is closing."

Somebody responded, "You can make things better, yessirree. Jack can."

I looked up to see Crazy Coote jabbing his finger toward me and nodding to make his point. "Jack Hicks can make things better, yessirree."

I just stared at him with my mouth hanging open as

he walked away, still talking. I didn't know Coote even knew my name.

He was right, though, just like he'd been right about the rain. I could make things better. *I will make things better*, I thought. The frogs at the tailings pond may be dead, but one survived. *This is the only frog in Coppertown, and it's up to me to make sure he's okay.*

When I got home, I placed him carefully in one of Mom's large mason jars then got to work.

"Jack, it's getting close to supper," she called from the den. "What are you doing?"

"I've got a project to finish up, Mom. I'll be out back."

Behind Dad's metal shop, I dug out my old aquarium. I had a tank full of guppies when I was young, but I hadn't known how to take care of things back then. It was caked with mud and took a while to scrub clean, but I didn't stop until it was perfect. The sun sank over the hills and cast long blue shadows across our backyard. I collected some dirt and gravel from the garden—the good soil, not the dead stuff—and set it in the bottom before carrying the aquarium inside.

In my bedroom, I cleared off the spot on the shelf in front of my window where I'd grown my seeds and placed the aquarium on it. I found a shallow screw-top lid in the kitchen, filled it with water, and placed it in the corner. It was bare, but it wasn't so different from the tailings pond, really. I fetched the mason jar and placed it on its side in the aquarium.

As if on cue, the little frog hopped out of the jar into his new home and chirped.

I smiled. "There's a lot countin' on you, little man."

Little Man, I thought. "I'll call you Little Man."

Just then, Mom poked her head into my room. "Jack, what are you up to?" She walked over. "A frog? Where on earth did you find a frog?"

I squinted at her apologetically. "The tailings pond," I said and braced for the teardown.

"Jack Hicks, it's dangerous up there!"

"Don't worry," I said. "I won't be goin' anymore. All the frogs are dead—the dumping killed them. Little Man here is the only one left." I told her the whole story, about the floodwaters and the frog eggs. How we watched them turn into tadpoles then frogs. By the end of it, tears were runnin' down my face again.

"I am not happy you were up there, Jack Hicks, and

for that, you're grounded until I say otherwise," she said, then put her arm around me. "But you did a good thing saving Little Man here. What are you going to feed him?"

I looked at my amphibian book. "Crickets, I think."

"Well, that's easy enough," she said. "You can pick some up from Pa's bait shop tomorrow."

"I thought I was grounded."

"Well, mostly."

CHAPTER 31

Nests

The next day, after pickin' out the smallest crickets I could find at Grandpa's bait shop, I showed Piran my setup for Little Man.

"They were all dead?" he asked.

"All except for this guy."

"That really sucks." He plopped down on my bed.

"Yeah. I can't wait until the Company is gone for good," I said and placed a tiny cricket in the aquarium. Instinct took over, and it didn't take long for Little Man to find it.

"But the town needs the Company," Piran argued.

"It needs something," I replied, "but not that."

Little Man croaked happily.

"You should've seen those scabs the other day," I said. "They looked mean."

"You'll have a cool scar from the rock they threw at

you," Piran replied. His version of the story was already growin'. I grimaced and didn't bother correcting him.

"Dad hit the roof when he heard about Eli crossing the picket line," Piran said. "I can't imagine what he'd do if he knew about the pot."

"What about Hannah?"

"She sucked up to my parents and moved back in. We'll have *another* baby in the house soon. Can you believe it?"

I shook my head.

"Have you heard from your dad?" Piran asked.

"He called last night, but it's long distance, so I didn't get to talk to him."

"Well, when are they comin' home?"

"I dunno," I said. "Supposedly, there's a whole bunch of people waiting to talk to the supervisor."

Just then, the phone rang in the kitchen. Piran and I jumped. I ran down the hall. As I came around the corner, Mom was walking toward me with a huge smile spreading across her face. "Jack, your dad's coming home this afternoon."

"Any news?" I asked.

"He wouldn't say," she replied, but she didn't stop smiling.

She grabbed her purse, riffled through it, and pulled out a ten-dollar bill. "Here." She handed it to me.

"What's this?" I asked.

"Why don't you and Piran go see a movie," Mom said and looked at the clock. "There should be one starting in about forty minutes."

Piran and I exchanged a strange look. "Really? But what about Dad comin' home?"

"Don't worry. He'll be here when you get back. Now go on, you two. Shoo." She practically pushed us out the door. "Go have fun."

"Ever feel like you're not wanted?" Piran said as we crossed the yard.

"Yeah." I laughed. "Don't let the door hit ya on the way out." Still, I wasn't going to complain. My parents hadn't given me money for the movies in ages.

Some of the other miners' kids were already at the theater when we got there. *Weird*, I thought. They all oohed over the bandage on my forehead after Piran told them the story of the picket line—extremely exaggerated, of course.

Since most of the kids were still in middle school and Piran and I were gonna be in high school soon, we took charge. We handled everybody's ticket purchases and then bought ourselves an enormous bucket of popcorn. I inhaled the hot butter and salt as we entered the dark theater. I didn't even care what movie we were going to see. I was just glad to be there.

I'd eaten about half our bucket when Piran started the popcorn fight. Mr. Mabely tried to get us to settle down. "You kids hush up or I'll kick you out!" But I saw a smile sneak across his face as he turned to leave.

We drank our Cherry Cokes too fast and had a burping contest. Piran won by a mile.

We missed most of the movie, sure, but we had a great time.

It was late afternoon when we left the theater. I checked the lamppost for the sparrow, but it wasn't there.

All the way home I tried to brace myself for whatever news my dad might have. *Did he get a job? Will we have to move?*

I ran into the house, slamming the screen door. "Dad!" I yelled, but it was dark and quiet, except for Bill Monroe's "In the Pines" driftin' from the kitchen radio. I hummed along with the chorus: "In the pines, in the pines, where the sun never shines."

Nothin' like that here, I thought. *Not yet anyhow.*

I walked down the hallway looking for my parents. Dust motes drifted through the setting sun as it filtered through the windows. "Mom? Dad?"

Still no answer.

I went out back and finally found my parents smooching between sheets drying on the clothesline.

"Ew!"

Mom reached out and held my hand. "Jack, your dad got a job." She beamed.

I held my breath. "Do we have to move?" I asked.

"It's a long way to go every day," Dad said, "but the men and I will take turns drivin'. We can do it."

I smiled so big, I thought my face would break in two.

Just then, sunlight flickered across my eyes. There was the sparrow again, perched on the laundry pole with a twig in its beak.

"What do you know," Dad said.

I blinked at the setting sun that framed the bird from behind and watched as it flew from the pole to my dogwood tree, where it wove the twig into its brand-new nest.

"Maybe we could pick up a bird feeder at the Piggly Wiggly next time we go," Mom said.

"You'll need birdseed too," Dad replied.

I nodded and smiled even bigger, if that was possible.

While Mom made supper, Dad and I sat on the porch swing and stared at the Company. Its familiar silhouette was already startin' to change. Some of the pipes stretched out and met nothing but air, and a few of the holding tanks were already gone. Parts were leaving by train and truck, never to return. I was thrilled it was coming down.

"There was an article in the paper about what Tom Hill said—that they're moving the whole thing down to South America. No unions down there. I imagine it'll be much like it used to be here," Dad said. "They'll have to fight for fair treatment, just like we did."

"It's not right." I frowned and thought about what Grandpa had said: *Life is like that sometimes.*

The red-and-white-striped smokestack still stood. I wondered if they'd leave it as some kind of memorial.

"I suppose the mining days in Coppertown are officially over," Dad said.

I took a deep breath. It was time to tell him. "Dad, I know you wanted me to, and it was the family tradition and all, but... But I never wanted to be a miner," I said. "I'm sorry." I shut my lips tight and waited.

He looked at me long and hard. "What do you want to be, then?"

"A forest ranger," I said. "I want to bring the trees back to Coppertown."

"A forest ranger, huh?" He sat staring straight ahead for the longest time. "Seems like you'd need to go to college for somethin' like that."

"I suppose so," I muttered.

"You'd have to get scholarships and work your way through. I couldn't afford to send you," he said. "But you'd be the first one in this family to get past high school. You want it bad enough?"

I gulped and smiled. "Yup. I want it bad enough."

He patted me on the shoulder. "I think you'd be real good at that, Jack."

I felt fifty pounds lighter.

The miners picked Dad up early the next morning to go work at the new carpet mill.

Mom and I stood in the yard to send him off right. Just before he left, Dad pressed the fairy cross into my hand.

"It brought me luck, Jack," he said. "Thanks."

CHAPTER 32

Trees

Piran was happy to hear the news too. "I guess I won't be the last kid in Coppertown after all." He smiled and punched my arm.

We fished all morning, but my mind was someplace else. I was so happy, I was flying, just like that sparrow. We didn't have to move. We weren't going anywhere, but the Company was. With it gone, nature actually stood a chance. The trees could come back, but they needed help. I thought about my garden and wondered how hard it would be to plant a garden the size of Coppertown.

"We gotta go to the post office this afternoon," Piran said. "My dad's gettin' a big shipment of baby chickens in. The Miller family is gonna start farming. Can you believe it?"

"That'll be somethin' to see," I replied.

When we got there, people were walkin' out with wide smiles. The second we opened the door, we understood why. The sound of squawks and peeps was deafening.

"What a madhouse!" Mr. Quinn said and threw up his hands. "It's impossible to get any work done today."

Behind him sat stacks and stacks of short boxes. Little beaks and furry yellow wings poked out of the holes that lined the sides. The containers shook from the baby chickens shuffling around inside. Piran and I stretched over the counter as far as possible to get a better look.

As I reached, I accidentally knocked a stack of flyers off the counter, sending them fluttering to the ground.

"Oops, sorry, Mr. Quinn." I knelt down to gather the mess. That's when I noticed what was printed at the top of each paper in bold black letters:

TREE PLANTERS WANTED
for CERP
(Coppertown Environmental Reclamation Project)
Pay: 10¢ per seedling planted
Call...

I stopped breathing and my eyes watered. "No way," I whispered. I could barely speak. "Mr. Quinn, are these for everybody?" I asked as I returned the untidy stack to the counter. I tried to straighten it, but I was so excited that my hands were shaking.

"Sure, Jack," he replied. "A man from some environmental agency dropped them off this morning."

"Piran, I gotta go," I said.

"What the...?"

"I'll talk to you later!" I called out as I grabbed a flyer from the top of the stack and ran out the door. I whooped and hollered and waved that flyer above my head like a victory flag all the way home.

Author's Note

While *A Bird on Water Street* is fiction, Jack's story weaves through a real time and place in American history. Coppertown is based on the real town of Copperhill, Tennessee, located in what's called the Copper Basin, where Georgia, Tennessee, and North Carolina meet at the southern gateway to the Appalachian Mountains.

Copper was discovered in the area in 1843, not long after the Cherokee and other Native Americans were forced to walk the Trail of Tears. Tin miners were brought in from Cornwall, England, as well as other countries, to apply their expertise to copper mining, which ran almost continuously until 1986.

Life was crazier than the Wild West in those days. The remote area was cut off from most of civilization by rocky terrain and terrible roads. Before the railroad, wagons (pulled by teams of donkeys or oxen) typically took weeks to haul supplies and copper in and out of the mountains. Therefore, miners turned to the locally available fuel to keep the smelters running—wood.

By the 1870s, more than fifty square miles of land had been stripped completely bare of trees. Toxic fumes of sulfur dioxide expelled from heaps of roasting ore created acid rain, which killed off everything else. The area remained devoid of vegetation for more than a hundred years. While some reclamation efforts began as early as 1929, most of the land was not successfully reclaimed until 1981. In the 1800s, the long-term effects of mining on the environment were considered acceptable.

Sometimes that collateral damage included loss of life. But mining was lucrative, as, over time, Americans grew to rely on the products made from the mined materials—electrical wiring, roof shingles, pool cleaners, detergent, fertilizer, and even toothpaste.

I have long been drawn to the Appalachian Mountains: as a child visiting my grandparents in Lexington, Virginia; at camp in Mentone, Alabama; as an instructor at the John C. Campbell Folk School in Murphy, North Carolina; and as a Professor at Hollins University in Roanoke,

Virginia. I can't stay away. So, it was a dream come true when my husband and I moved to a cabin in the North Georgia mountains in 2001.

We landed just south of Copperhill where I stood many times with a foot on each side of the state line in the IGA Grocery Store parking lot. Ironically, I'd driven through the area many times over the years while on the way to go camping. Back then, the devastation to the land was still visible. As we drove by, we'd wave our support to striking miners who sat in front of what we called 'the rape of the land'—miles of bare soil and no other living things.

Living in the Copper Basin, there was no avoiding the complicated history and the impact the mining had on the community. One night we were invited to a town hall meeting where they were discussing the possibility of opening a new scenic railway that would run north from the town, around an unusual corkscrew track, and then return to Copperhill. (One already existed going south of town to Blue Ridge, and it was a successful tourist attraction.) To fund the endeavor, the plant wanted to send out one shipment of sulfuric acid a week. It meant jobs, but it also meant a return of the toxins that had taken such a toll on the citizens.

Former miners stood like gnarled oak trees in

their plaid flannel shirts and denim overalls and shared horrendous stories of entire crews that died from cancers believed to be caused by the mines. They threatened to sabotage the tracks if plans moved forward. I couldn't believe what I'd stumbled into.

The story grabbed hold of me that night and demanded to be written—by me. But I wasn't a local, I wasn't a miner. I had to tread carefully on what was obviously hallowed ground. I immersed myself in uncomfortable research and learned the details of 150 years of mining history. A lot of it was ugly and disturbing, but I needed to know it to tell the story.

I also did countless interviews. At first, people were wary of my inquiries, but when Grace Postelle and Doris Abernathy became my friends, they opened doors for me. Grace and Doris were eighty-year-old sisters who grew up in Copperhill, and they were somewhat legendary. It was Grace who told me the original story of Helen McKay who saw a bird on Water Street in the 1920s, inspiring the book's title. And it was Doris who saw the story through to completion with so many of her own stories woven throughout.

As people shared their history, I learned to keep an open mind. For some, the red-and-white-striped smokestack was a beloved symbol of the town. Others loved their "red hills"—imagine growing up in a place with no bugs, no snakes, no poison ivy, and no allergies! And yet, the acid rain stung and the air often smelled like rotten eggs. The wind was too corrosive for tin roofs (everybody had asphalt shingles) and, I was told, could eat up a pair of nylon stockings hanging on a clothesline in a matter of minutes.

The entire town's economy relied upon the Company—from the housing, to the grocery store, to the schools. Mining was considered good work with high pay and benefits, but it was dangerous work. The miners had to fight for unions, which helped improve health and safety standards for the workers. However, the Environmental Protection Agency (EPA) allowed for some exposure to toxins to be legal, and they often received reports that regulations were not being followed.

Cancer was rampant. I was told a story about three men from the same mining crew who all died from pancreatic cancer in the same year. While the connection between mining and poor health was never technically proven, it seemed too obvious to be coincidence.

Life in the Copper Basin was challenging to both

the land and the people. I wondered how I could take all that good and bad and wrap it into a story that people would want to read. I decided to compress the story into one year, as historical fiction told through the eyes of an innocent—thirteen-year-old Jack Hicks. Just as Jack questions his world, I hope you, as the reader, experience his confusion and wonder alongside him. It was through Jack that I was able to relay the extensive damage, and the strong and unified community that lived through it. Jack became the voice of everyman.

The closing of the Company occurs quickly in *A Bird on Water Street*, but in reality, the closing of the mine took over a decade. In 1985, the Company announced copper mining would be phased out, and thousands of men were laid off over the following years. Mining operations halted completely in 1987 even though sulfuric acid production continued well into the 1990s. Some laid-off workers ended up striking for as long as ten years.

Copperhill did experience a small boon during the 1996 Summer Olympics when the white-water competitions were held downstream on the Ocoee (Tohachee) River. It was a shining moment for the residents and changed the focus of the town, which now relies on tourist dollars to survive. Visitors enjoy the old scenic railway that runs south to Blue Ridge, the vacation log cabins, and what is now a beautiful vista.

Eventually, the sulfuric acid plant was sold to a company in Brazil. Out-of-town contractors were brought in to start tearing the plant down just before my husband and I moved away in 2005. It seemed yet another slight against the local people who could have used the work.

Although reclamation efforts began as early as the 1930s with President Franklin D. Roosevelt's New Deal plan and the Civilian Conservation Corps (the CCC), they simply didn't have an impact until the early 1990s when sulfuric acid production was finally halted. By the time my husband and I moved to the region in 2001, most of the area had been reforested, although signs of the previous damage were still visible in some places, especially around the tailings ponds.

Much of the local history is preserved at the Ducktown Basin Museum, where visitors can see truly shocking photos of the once-denuded landscape and schedule tours of the tailings ponds to observe reclamation efforts firsthand. Ironically, much of the region is now wetlands. Reeds and grasses act as nature's filtration process and now cover the once-polluted area.

Wildlife is slowly returning, even frogs.

Along with a complicated history, the Appalachian Mountains are home to a fascinating culture. Because of their inaccessibility, mountain communities evolved independent from outside influences, becoming living examples of their European—most notably Celtic—ancestry. It influenced their stories and especially their music, which was the foundation for today's bluegrass. The thick Elizabethan dialects, long lost to the rest of the world, could make a voice sound like a bagpipe with a long continuous drawl. And whereas most Southerners say "y'all," in the mountains they say "yu'uns."

"The Jack Tales" are an important part of Jack Hicks's story as well as mine. Rooted in European fairy tales like "Jack and the Beanstalk," the stories changed and adapted in the Appalachian Mountains and became tales wholly American. The epicenter of the Jack Tales was on Beech Mountain in North Carolina where Ray Hicks (August 29, 1922–August 20, 2003) lived and was named a national treasure as Keeper of the Jack Tales. I was lucky to hear him tell those tales in person on several occasions at the National Storytelling Festival in Jonesborough, Tennessee. For more on my personal history with

Jack Tales, visit my blog, dulemba.blogspot.com and search "Jack Tales."

While living in the Copper Basin, my husband and I had the privilege to meet some true mountain folks, great-great-grandsons and great-great-granddaughters of the miners who had such an impact on the history there. We were touched by the loyalty and openness we found once we'd been accepted as friends. We were graced with their hospitality, their stories, and especially their music.

When the first edition of *A Bird on Water Street* was released in 2014, I had the great pleasure of sharing the book with the Appalachian community from Benton, Tennessee, to Blue Ridge, Georgia. I was humbled and honored to have created something that became bigger than myself, something that the local people were proud of and claimed as a valued representation of their history.

Even more than that, I was honored to create a story that makes people think and perhaps become better stewards of the earth and our precious resources in the future.

The Copper Basin

C opper mining in the Southern Appalachians began in 1843 and ran almost continuously until 1986. While there were several companies operating, two main companies were in control of the basin during the late nineteenth century to early twentieth century—the Ducktown Sulfur, Copper & Iron Company (headquarter in Isabella, Tennessee) and the Tennessee Copper Company (headquarter in Copperhill, Tennessee). Together, they owned and operated ten separate ore bodies, or mines, in the area. Eventually the Tennessee Copper Company bought Ducktown in 1936.

The ore bodies contained iron, zinc, and copper sulfides, but prior to 1909, both companies only had the technology to remove the copper from the ground. The iron and zinc were dumped in the slag (or waste) from copper smelting. By the 1920s, all three metals were being extracted from the ore bodies in the basin.

By the 1870s, the Copper Basin was stripped completely bare of trees, and the toxic fumes of sulfur dioxide created acid rain, which killed off the remaining vegetation. The area remained devoid of vegetation for over a hundred years. While some reclamation efforts began as early as 1929, most of the land was not successfully reclaimed until 1981.

Images from the Copper Basin

▲ The Ducktown Sulfur, Copper & Iron Company's smelting works, circa 1890s. The plant's headquarters were in Isabella, Tennessee, and sat at the junction of two hollows.

▲ The DSC&IC train up front is carrying ore waiting to be smelted or quartz, which was used to help the smelters run smoothly.

▲ A section of the plant in Isabella, Tennessee, circa 1920s. The train moved ore from the DSC&IC mines for copper extraction. Miner homes and the Union Methodist Church are in the background. The church also served as a school building, and has a "spirit hole" similar to the one Jack noticed during Mrs. Ledford's funeral.

◄ Aerial view of the Mary Mine and Mill, owned by the DSC&IC, circa 1920. Visible are the mill (center), various support and supply buildings, and a few miner residences.

▲ Miners running a machine drill to create tunnels for ore extraction. Being a driller was a high-paying job and one of the best in the mines. In the nineteenth century, drilling was done by hand, holding a piece of steel against the rock and hitting it with a hammer.

◄ The technology used in the Copper Basin mines was innovative for its time, although by today's standards it was very dangerous. The danger was twofold—running the machine in such an enclosed space meant a miner was at risk of injury either from the machine itself or from rocks falling from overhead.

▲ Miners in front of a "grizzly," where ore cars are loaded from different sections of the mine. They are standing on the twentieth level, which was about two thousand feet below ground.

▲ Tennessee Copper Company in Copperhill, Tennessee, circa 1943. About one-third of the surrounding towns of Copperhill, McCaysville, Ducktown, and Isabella worked for the Company.

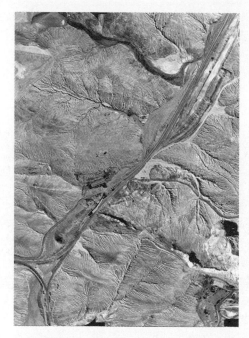

◄ Aerial view of the McPherson area in 1944. The McPherson mine is in the center, surrounded by some of the rail lines and roads that connect the site to other mines. The upper left corner shows a portion of a tailings pond and the small cracks along the land are gullies from erosion. The larger cracks are "cuts," or the exposed tops of ore deposits, where mining could once be done from the surface instead of going underground. Notice how bare the landscape is— there were no trees, no bugs, and no birds for fifty square miles.

▲ Houses miners would rent from the Company. These homes were abandoned, and families were moved to new homes, after a section of the Boyd Mine collapsed in the early 1960s.

1980

2004

◄ The Burra Burra mine collapse from the viewing platform at the Ducktown Basin Museum in Ducktown, TN, showing the progression of nature moving back in over time. The area around the collapse was intentionally unreclaimed because of the danger of a further cave-in, but also because it shows a clear "before" and "after" contrast to appreciate.

2012

Acknowledgments

Most of Jack's experiences have a thread of truth running through them; they were gathered through interviews spanning nearly a decade.

For helping me gather history, stories, and flavor, as well as offering their friendship, I'd especially like to thank: sisters Grace Postelle and Doris Abernathy, without whom I could not have written this book; Howard Slaughter; John Quinn; Leland Rymer; Mathew Maloof (he and his friends used to jump off trestle bridges when the trains came); Greg Barker (his father, Gene Barker, was one of the last three men—along with Danny "Red" Dilbeck and Eugene Trammell—out of the copper mines when they closed, before the tunnels were flooded to prevent future collapses); Toni and Walter Bahn; Lynne and Jim Jones; Lisa and Brad Waggoner; Debbie and J. Hammock; John Thomas; Dick and Judy Spencer; Kay Kendall; Tina Hanlon; the Three Wise Men (the inspiration for Coote); Richard McCay Wagner; and finally, Mrs. Helen McCay Wagner (1912–1996), who originally saw that bird on Water Street in 1924.

I'd like to thank my writerly friends—those subjected to early drafts or who helped with sound writing advice: Vicky Alvear Shecter, Karin Slaughter, Jen Weiss Handler, Jessica Handler, Courtney Miller-Callihan, Lisa Jacobi, Kirby Larson, Jennifer Jabaley, and my dear friend Liz Conrad (may she rest in peace).

For helping me with accuracy and information while writing *A Bird on Water Street*, I'd like to thank: Ken Rush, the director of the Ducktown Basin Museum; Dawna Standridge, Shelby Standridge Sisson, and Joyce Allen, also of the museum; Nick Wimberley, former secretary/treasurer and negotiator for the International Brotherhood of Boilermakers; Alan Gratz for baseball specifics; Mia Manekofsky for genre guidance; Rod Walton, Lisa Ganser, and Fred Ming for information about frogs; Lou Laux and Tom Striker for information on birds; and former Fannin County sheriff George Ensley for research about cannabis-growing in the Appalachians. The sparrow song description was found in *American Birds in Color*, written by Hal H. Harrison (New York: Wm. H. Wise & Co., Inc., 1948).

Any mistakes made in this book are wholly my own in my attempt to relay the feeling of the place, time, and events rather than exact facts. As they say, "Never let the truth get in the way of a good story." As such, I must thank my readers, the librarians, and residents of the tristate region who supported the first release of *A Bird on Water Street*. During the initial book tour, I heard even more of their amazing stories about the history of the area and was humbled to learn that I made them proud.

I'd like to thank the barrel of pickles at Little Pickle Press who published the first edition of *A Bird on Water Street*: Rana DiOrio, Dani Greer, Molly Glover, Julie Romeis Sanders, Cameron Crane, Kelly Wickham, Heather Lennon, and especially my editor Tanya Egan Gibson, who made the book truly shine.

And I'd like to thank the good folks at Sourcebooks, the new home for *A Bird on Water Street*, for believing in the story and breathing new life into its design and outreach: Kelly Barrales-Saylor, Bunmi Ishola, Michelle Lecuyer, Eliza Smith, Travis Hasenour, and Jordan Kost. It takes a village to raise a child, and it takes an inspired team of people to create a book that endures. I am forever grateful to you all.

Last, but certainly not least, I'd like to thank Stan.

I am lucky to have a husband who believes in me, my craft, and my crazy ideas. Without his support, I would not be the creator I am today. Love you, sweetie.

Discussion Questions

1. How would you describe Jack? How is he similar to and/or different from his dad, his mom, and Piran? Which character did you relate to the most, and what was it about them that you connected with?

2. Describe Coppertown. What makes the setting unique or important to the story? How does the setting help to shape Jack's life and define him as a character? How does the setting shape other characters and their experiences?

3. The author did a lot of research on the Copper Basin to help create authentic setting, events, and characters. Look through the book for details that seem to reflect facts. What are the most interesting facts you learned about the region and everyday life in Tennessee Appalachia?

4. Jack comes from a long line of copper miners. Both of his grandfathers were miners, and his uncles and dad are miners. How do Jack's feelings about being a miner differ from his dad's? Are there any members of Jack's family who feel the same as he does about the mines?

5. Many things that we use every day (like toothpaste) start with copper mining. Do you think there are some products that excuse the damage that comes from mining? Are there items you'd be willing to live without?

6. Mining isn't the only human activity that has led to environmental devastation. Can you think of other ways our actions have destroyed the environment? Are there any examples near where you live?

7. When the author was interviewing locals who grew up in the "red hills" like Jack, many of them were quite proud of the barren landscape and loved it. Can you make positive arguments for the ruined landscape?

8. When things started going wrong for the miners, they turned to the Union for help. What were the

goals they hoped the Union would achieve? Do you think the Union was successful? What challenges did the Union face?

9. When the miners go on strike and the mines stop production, Jack begins to notice a lot of change in Coppertown. What are some of the positive effects of the mines being closed? What are some of the negative effects?

10. At the end of the book, Jack's father and his crew are able to find work at a carpet mill over an hour away from Coppertown. What did you think about them choosing to stay in town and drive that far for work? How do you think this solution will help or hurt Jack's family? How might it hurt or help Coppertown?

11. What are some of the ways Jack tries to help his family, his community, and the environment throughout the book? Does Jack actually have the power to bring change? What would you do to help if you were in a similar situation?

12. How does the book's title relate to its contents? If you could give it a new title, what might you choose?

13. What do you think is the big takeaway message from *A Bird on Water Street*?

14. Do you think that *A Bird on Water Street* is ultimately a story of hope? Why or why not?

15. Do you think this book can or will change the way people think about and treat the environment? Why or why not?

About the Author

Elizabeth O. Dulemba is an award-winning author, illustrator, teacher, and speaker (including a TEDx talk). She has more than two dozen books to her credit, most recently illustrating *New York Times* bestselling author Jane Yolen's *MerBaby's Lullaby* and *On Eagle Cove*. Her debut novel, *A Bird on Water Street* has garnered fourteen literary awards and honors, including Georgia Author of the Year and a Green Earth Book Award Honor.

Elizabeth holds a BFA in graphic design from the University of Georgia and an MFA in illustration from the University of Edinburgh. She is continuing her PhD research in children's literature at the University of Glasgow (Scotland) while starting a new position as associate professor of illustration at Winthrop University in Rock Hill, South Carolina. In the summers, she travels to Roanoke, Virginia, where she is visiting associate professor at Hollins University in the low-residency MFA program in writing and illustrating children's books.

Elizabeth spent several years as illustrator coordinator for the southern region of the Society of Children's Book Writers and Illustrators (SCBWI), and as a board member for the Georgia Center for the Book. Prior to her career in children's literature, she was a corporate art director and in-house illustrator for packaging, apparel, and communications firms. She grew up in the American South; lived in Edinburgh, Scotland, for four years; and now lives in Rock Hill, South Carolina, with her husband, Stan.

Visit dulemba.com to learn more and sign up for "e's news."